Praise for RITA Award–winning author
Karen Marie Moning and her novels

"Rife with unexpected plot twists, Druid lore and sparkling humor . . . There's much that's fun here, both in characters and situations . . . Moning's snappy prose, quick wit, and charismatic characters will enchant."　—*Publishers Weekly*

"Enough sexual tension here to fuel a half dozen normal romances."　　　　　　　　　—*The Contra Costa Times*

"Moning is quickly building a reputation for writing poignant time travels with memorable characters."
　　　　　　　　　　　　　　　　—*The Oakland Press*

"A sensuous treat."　　　　　　　　　　　　—*Booklist*

"Highly original . . . sensual, hard-to-put-down romance. Karen Marie Moning is destined to make her mark on the genre."　　　　　　　　　　　　　—*Romantic Times*

"A great romantic fantasy . . . one of the best writers on the market today."　　　　　　　—*Midwest Book Review*

"Ms. Moning stretches our imagination, sending us flying into the enchanting past."　　　　　　—*Rendezvous*

"Seductive, mesmerizing, and darkly sensual."
　　　　　　　　　　　　　　　　—*Library Journal*

"Nonstop action for fans of paranormal romance."
　　　　　　　　　　　　　　　　—*Kirkus Reviews*

Into the Dreaming

Karen Marie Moning

JOVE BOOKS, NEW YORK

THE BERKLEY PUBLISHING GROUP
Published by the Penguin Group
Penguin Group (USA) Inc.
375 Hudson Street, New York, New York 10014, USA

Penguin Group (Canada), 90 Eglinton Avenue East, Suite 700, Toronto, Ontario M4P 2Y3, Canada
(a division of Pearson Penguin Canada Inc.)
Penguin Books Ltd., 80 Strand, London WC2R 0RL, England
Penguin Group Ireland, 25 St. Stephen's Green, Dublin 2, Ireland (a division of Penguin Books Ltd.)
Penguin Group (Australia), 250 Camberwell Road, Camberwell, Victoria 3124, Australia
(a division of Pearson Australia Group Pty. Ltd.)
Penguin Books India Pvt. Ltd., 11 Community Centre, Panchsheel Park, New Delhi—110 017, India
Penguin Group (NZ), Cnr. Airborne and Rosedale Roads, Albany, Auckland 1310, New Zealand
(a division of Pearson New Zealand Ltd.)
Penguin Books (South Africa) (Pty.) Ltd., 24 Sturdee Avenue, Rosebank, Johannesburg 2196,
South Africa

Penguin Books Ltd., Registered Offices: 80 Strand, London WC2R 0RL, England

Previously published in the anthology *Tapestry,* published by Jove Publications, Inc.

This is a work of fiction. Names, characters, places, and incidents either are the product of the author's imagination or are used fictitiously, and any resemblance to actual persons, living or dead, business establishments, events, or locales is entirely coincidental. The publisher does not have any control over and does not assume any responsibility for author or third-party websites or their content.

INTO THE DREAMING

A Jove Book / published by arrangement with the author.

PRINTING HISTORY
Jove mass-market edition / September 2006

Copyright © 2002, 2006 by Karen Marie Moning.

ISBN: 0-515-14150-X

JOVE®
Jove Books are published by The Berkley Publishing Group,
a division of Penguin Group (USA) Inc.,
375 Hudson Street, New York, New York 10014.
JOVE is a registered trademark of Penguin Group (USA) Inc.
The "J" design is a trademark belonging to Penguin Group (USA) Inc.

PRINTED IN THE UNITED STATES OF AMERICA

10 9 8 7 6 5 4 3 2 1

For my sister Laura, whose talent for shaping unformed clay extends to far more than that which can be fired in a kiln.
May your gardens ever bloom in lush profusion,
May your peach jam and pecan chicken always taste like heaven,
May the artistry inside your soul always find expression,
And may you always know how loved you are.

His hard, wet body glistened in the moonlight as he emerged from the ocean. Brilliant eyes of stormy aquamarine met hers, and her heart raced.

He stood naked before her, the look in his eyes offering everything, promising eternity.

When he cupped one strong hand at the nape of her neck and drew her closer to receive his kiss, her lips parted on a sigh of dreamy anticipation.

His kiss was at first gentle, then as stormy as the man himself, for he was a man of deep secrets, a man of deeper passion, her Highlander.

One hand became two buried in her hair, one kiss became a second of fierce and fiery desire, then he swept her into his arms, raced up the castle steps, and carried her to his bedchamber . . .

Excerpted from the unpublished manuscript
Highland Fire by Jane Sillee

One

It was a land of shadows and ice.

Of gray. And grayer. And black.

Deep in the shadows lurked inhuman creatures, twisted of limb and hideous of countenance. Things one did well to avoid seeing.

Should the creatures enter the pale bars of what passed for light in the terrible place, they would die, painfully and slowly. As would he—the mortal Highlander imprisoned within columns of sickly light—should he succeed in breaking the chains that held him and seek escape through those terrifying shadows.

Jagged cliffs of ice towered above him. A frigid wind shrieked through dark labyrinthine canyons, bearing a susurrus of desolate voices and faint, hellish screams. No

sun, no fair breeze of Scotland, no scent of heather pen-
etrated his frozen, bleak hell.

He hated it. His very soul cringed at the horror of the
place.

He ached for the warmth of the sun on his face and
hungered for the sweet crush of grass beneath his boots.
He would have given years of his life for the surety of
his stallion between his thighs and the solid weight of his
claymore in his grip.

He dreamed—when he managed to escape the agony
of his surroundings by retreating deep into his mind—of
the blaze of a peat fire, scattered with sheaves of heather.
Of a woman's warm, loving caresses. Of buttery, golden-
crusted bread hot from the hearth. Simple things. Impossible things.

For the son of a Highland chieftain, who'd passed a
score and ten in resplendent mountains and vales, five
years was an intolerable sentence; an incarceration that
would be withstood only by force of will, by careful nur-
turing of the light of hope within his heart.

But he was a strong man, with the royal blood of Scottish kings running hot and true in his veins. He would
survive. He would return and reclaim his rightful place,
woo and win a bonny lass with a tender heart and a tem-
pestuous spirit like his mother, and fill the halls of Dun
Haakon with the music of wee ones.

With such dreams, he withstood five years in the hellish
wasteland.

Only to discover the dark king had deceived him.

His sentence had never been five years at all, but five
fairy years: five hundred years in the land of shadow and
ice.

On that day when his heart turned to ice within his
breast, on that day when a single tear froze upon his
cheek, on that day when he was denied even the simple
solace of dreaming, he came to find his prison a place of
beauty.

*   *   *

"My queen, the Unseelie king holds a mortal captive."

The Seelie queen's face remained impassive, lest her court see how deeply disturbing she found the messenger's news. Long had the Seelie Court of Light and the Unseelie Court of Dark battled. Long had the Unseelie king provoked her. "Who is this mortal?" she asked coolly.

"Aedan MacKinnon, son and heir of the Norse princess Saucy Mary and Findanus MacKinnon, from Dun Haakon on the Isle of Skye."

"Descendent of the Scottish king, Kenneth McAlpin," the queen mused aloud. "The Unseelie king grows greedy, his aim lofty, if he seeks to turn the seed of the McAlpin to his dark ways. What bargain did he strike with this mortal?"

"He sent his current Hand of Vengeance into the world to bring death to the mortal's clansmen yet bartered that if the mortal willingly consented to spend five years in his kingdom, he would spare his kin."

"And the MacKinnon agreed?"

"The king concealed from him that five years in Faery is five centuries. Still, as grandseed of the McAlpin, I suspect the MacKinnon would have accepted the full term to protect his clan."

"What concession does the king make?" the queen asked shrewdly. Any bargain between fairy and mortal must hold the possibility for the human to regain his freedom. Still, no mortal had ever bested a fairy in such a bargain.

"At the end of his sentence, he will be granted one full cycle of the moon in the mortal world, at his home at Dun Haakon. If, by the end of that time, he is loved and loves in return, he will be free. If not, he serves as the king's new Hand of Vengeance until the king chooses to replace him, at which time he dies."

The queen made a sound curiously like a sigh. By such cruel methods had the Unseelie king long fashioned his deadly, prized assassin—his beloved Vengeance—by capturing a mortal, driving him past human limits into madness, indurating him to all emotion, then endowing him with special powers and arts.

Since the Unseelie king was barred entrance to the human world, he trained his Vengeance to carry out his orders, to hold no act too heinous. Mortals dared not even whisper the icy assassin's name, lest they inadvertently draw his merciless attention. If a man angered the Unseelie king, Vengeance punished the mortal's clan, sparing no innocents. If grumblings about the fairy were heard, Vengeance silenced them in cruelly imaginative ways. If the royal house was not amenable to the fairy world, Vengeance toppled kings as carelessly as one might sweep a chessboard.

Until now, it had been the Unseelie king's wont to abduct an insignificant mortal, one without clan who would not be missed, to train as his Vengeance. He went too far this time, the Seelie queen brooded, abducting a blood grandson of one of fair Scotia's greatest kings—a man of great honor, noble and true of heart.

She would win this mortal back.

The queen was silent for a time. Then, "Ah, what five hundred years in that place will do to him," she breathed in a chill voice. The Unseelie king had named the terms of his bargain well. Aedan MacKinnon would still be mortal at the end of his captivity but no longer remotely human when released. Once, long ago and never forgotten, she'd traversed that forbidden land herself, danced upon a pinnacle of black ice, slept within the dark king's velvet embrace . . .

"Perhaps an enchanted tapestry," she mused, "to bring the MacKinnon the one true mate to his heart." She could not fight the Unseelie king directly, lest the clash of their magic too gravely damage the land. But she could and would do all in her power to ensure Aedan MacKinnon found love at the end of his imprisonment.

"My queen," the messenger offered hesitantly, "they shall have but one bridge of the moon in the sky. Perhaps they should meet in the Dreaming."

The queen pondered a moment. The Dreaming: that elusive, much-sought, everforgotten realm where mortals occasionally brushed pale shoulder to iridescent wing with the fairy. That place where mortals would be astonished to know battles were won and lost, universes born, and true love preordained, from Cleopatra and Marc Antony to Abelard and Heloise. The lovers could meet in the Dreaming and share a lifetime of loving before they ever met in the mortal realm. It would lay a grand foundation for success of her plan.

"Wisely spoken," the queen agreed. Rising from her floral bower with fluid grace, she raised her arms and began to sing.

From her melody a tapestry was woven, of fairy lore, of bits of blood and bone, of silken hair from the great, great-grandson of the McAlpin, of ancient rites known only to the True Race. As she sang, her court chanted:

> *Into the Dreaming lure them deep*
> *where they shall love whilst they doth sleep*
> *then in the waking both shall dwell*
> *'til love's fire doth melt his ice-borne hell.*

And when the tapestry was complete, the queen marveled.

"Is this truly the likeness of Aedan MacKinnon?" she asked, eyeing the tapestry with unmistakable erotic interest.

"I have seen him, and it is so," the messenger replied, wetting his lips, his gaze fixed upon the tapestry.

"Fortunate woman," the queen said silkily.

*   *   *

The fairy queen went to him in the Dreaming, well into his sentence, when he was quite mad. Tracing a curved nail against his icy jaw, she whispered in his ear, "Hold fast, MacKinnon, for I have found you the mate to your soul. She will warm you. She will love you above all others."

The monster chained to the ice threw back his dark head and laughed.

It was not a human sound at all.

Two

Present day
Oldenburg, Indiana

Jane Sillee had an intensely passionate relationship with her postman.

It was classic love-hate.

The moment she heard him whistling his way down her walk, her heart kicked into overtime, a sappy smile curved her lips, and her breathing quickened.

But the moment he failed to deliver the acceptance letter extolling the wonders of her manuscript, or worse, handed her a rejection letter, she hated him. *Hated* him. Knew it was his fault somehow. That maybe, just maybe, a publisher had written glowing things about her, he'd dropped the letter because he was careless, the wind had picked it up and carried it off, and even now her bright and shining future lay sodden and decomposing in a mud puddle somewhere.

Just how much could a federal employee be trusted, anyway? she brooded suspiciously. He could be part of some covert study designed to determine how much one tortured writer could endure before snapping and turning into a pen-wielding felon.

"Purple prose, my ass," she muttered, balling up the latest rejection letter. "I only used black ink. I can't *afford* a color ink cartridge." She kicked the door of her tiny apartment shut and slumped into her secondhand nagahide recliner.

Massaging her temples, she scowled. She simply had to get this story published. She'd become convinced it was the only way she was ever going to get him out of her mind.

Him. Her sexy, dark-haired Highlander. The one who came to her in dreams.

She was hopelessly and utterly in love with him.

And at twenty-four, she was really beginning to worry about herself.

Sighing, she unballed and smoothed the rejection letter. This one was the worst of the lot and got pretty darned personal, detailing numerous reasons why her work was incompetent, unacceptable, and downright idiotic. "But I *do* hear celestial music when he kisses me," Jane protested. "At least in my dreams I do," she muttered.

Crumpling it again, she flung it across the room and closed her eyes.

Last night she'd danced with him, her perfect lover.

They'd waltzed in a woodland clearing, caressed by a fragrant forest breeze, beneath a black velvet canopy of glittering stars. She'd worn a gown of shimmering lemon-colored silk. He'd worn a plaid of crimson and black atop a soft, laced, linen shirt. His gaze had been so tender, so passionate, his hands so strong and masterful, his tongue so hot and hungry and—

Jane opened her eyes, sighing gustily. How was she supposed to have a normal life when she'd been dreaming about the man since she was old enough to remember dreaming? As a child, she'd thought him her guardian angel. But as she'd ripened into a young woman, he'd become so much more.

In her dreams, they'd skipped the dance of the swords between twin fires at Beltane atop a majestic mountain while sipping honeyed mead from pewter tankards. How could a cheesy high-school prom replete with silver disco ball suspended from the ceiling accompanied by plastic cups of Hawaiian Punch compare to that?

In her dreams, he'd deftly and with aching gentleness removed her virginity. Who wanted a Monday-night-football-watching, beer-drinking, insurance adjuster/frustrated wannabe-pro-golfer?

In her dreams he'd made love to her again and again, his heated touch shattering her innocence and awakening her to every manner of sensual pleasure. And although in her waking hours, she'd endeavored to lead a normal life, to fall for a flesh-and-blood man, quite simply, no mere man could live up to her dreams.

"You're hopeless. Get over him, already," Jane muttered to herself. If she had a dollar for every time she'd told herself that, she'd own Trump Tower. And the air rights above it.

Glancing at the clock, she pushed herself up from the chair. She was due at her job at the Smiling Cobra Café in twenty minutes, and if she was late again, Laura might make good on her threat to fire her. Jane had a tendency to forget the time, immersed in her writing or research or just plain daydreaming.

You're a throwback to some other era, Jane, Laura had said a dozen times.

And indeed, Jane had always felt she'd been born in the wrong century. She didn't own a car and didn't want one. She hated loud noises, condos, and skyscrapers and loved the unspoiled countryside and cozy cottages. She suffered living in an apartment because she couldn't afford a house. Yet.

She wanted her own vegetable garden and fruit orchard. Maybe a milking cow to make butter and cheese and fresh whipped cream. She longed to have babies—three boys and three girls would do nicely.

Yes, in this day and age, she was definitely a throwback. To cave man days, probably, she thought forlornly. When her girlfriends had graduated from college and rushed off with their business degrees and briefcases to work in steel-and-glass high-rises, determined to balance career, children, and marriage, Jane had taken her BA in English and gone to work in a coffee shop, harboring simpler aspirations. All she wanted was a low-pressure job that wouldn't interfere with her writing ambitions. Jane figured the skyrocketing divorce rate had a whole lot to do with people trying to tackle too much. Being a wife, lover, best friend, and mother seemed like a pretty full plate to her. And if—no, she amended firmly—*when* she finally got published, writing romance would be a perfect at-home career. She'd have the best of both worlds.

Right, and someday my prince will come . . .

Shrugging off an all-too-familiar flash of depression, she wheeled her bike out of the tiny hallway between the kitchen and bedroom and grabbed a jacket and her backpack. As she opened the door she glanced back over her shoulder to be sure she'd turned off her computer and ran smack into the large package that had been left on her doorstep.

That hadn't been there half an hour ago when she'd plucked her mail from the sweaty, untrustworthy hands of the postman. Perhaps he'd returned with it, she mused; it *was* large. It must be her recent Internet order from the online used bookstore, she decided. It was earlier than she'd anticipated, but she wasn't complaining.

She'd be blissfully immersed in larger-than-life heroes, steamy romance, and alternate universes for the next few days. Glancing at her watch again, she sighed, propped her bike against the doorjamb, dragged the box into her apartment, wheeled her bike back out into the hall, then shut and locked the door. She knew better than to open the box now. She'd quickly progress from stealing a quick glance at the covers, to opening a book, to getting completely lost in a fantasy world.

And then Laura would fire her for sure.

It was nearly one in the morning by the time Jane finally got home. If she'd had to make one more extra-shot, one-half decaf, Venti, double-cup, two-Sweet-n-Low, skim with light foam latte for one more picky, anorexic bimbo, she might have done bodily harm to a customer. Why couldn't anyone drink good old-fashioned coffee anymore? Heavy on the sugar—*loads* of cream. Life was too short to count calories. At least that's what she told herself each time the scale snidely deemed her plump for five-foot, three and three-quarter inches.

With a mental shrug, she scattered thoughts of work from her mind. It was over. She'd done her time, and now she was free to be just Jane. And she couldn't wait to start that new vampire romance she'd been dying to read!

After brushing her teeth, she slipped out of her jeans and sweater and into her favorite nightie, the frilly, romantic one with tiny daisies and cornflowers embroidered at the scooped neckline. She tugged the box near her bed before dropping cross-legged on the plump, old-fashioned feather ticks. Slicing the packing-tape seal with a metal nail file, she paused and sniffed, as an irresistibly spicy scent wafted from the box. Jasmine, sandalwood, and something else . . . something elusive that nudged her past feeling dreamily romantic to positively aroused. *Great time to read a romance,* she thought ruefully, *with no man to attack when the love scenes heat up*. Untouched except in her dreams, her hormones tended to simmer at a constant gentle boil.

With a wry smile, she dug past the purple Styrofoam peanuts and paused again when her hands closed on rough fabric. Frowning, she tugged it free, sending peanuts skittering across the hardwood floor. The exotic scent filled the room, and she glanced at the closed casement window, bemused by the sudden sultry breeze that lifted strands of her curly red hair and pressed her nightie close to her body.

Perplexed, she placed the folded fabric on her bed, then checked the box. No postmark, no return address, but her name was printed on the top in large block letters, next to her apartment number.

"Well, I'm not paying for it," she announced, certain a hefty bill would shortly follow. "I didn't order it." Darned if she was paying for something she didn't want. She had a hard enough time affording the things she did want.

Irritated that she had no new books to read, she plucked idly at the fabric, then unfolded it and spread it out on the bed.

And sat motionless, her mouth ajar.

"This is *not* funny," she breathed, shocked. "No," she amended in a shaky whisper, "this is not *possible*."

It was a tapestry, exquisitely woven of brilliant colors, featuring a magnificent Highland warrior standing before a medieval castle, legs spread in an arrogant stance that clearly proclaimed him master of the keep. Clad in a crimson and black tartan, adorned with clan regalia, both his hands were extended as if reaching for her.

And it was *him*. Her dream man.

Taking a deep breath, she closed her eyes, then opened them slowly.

It was still him. Each detail precisely as she'd dreamed him, from his powerful forearms and oh-so-capable hands to his luminous aqua eyes, to his silky dark hair and his sensual mouth.

How she would have loved living in medieval times, with a man like him!

Beneath his likeness, carefully stitched, was his name. "Aedan MacKinnon," she whispered.

Mortals did not bide captivity in Faery well—they did not age and time stretched into infinity—and Aedan MacKinnon was no exception. It took a mere two hundred years of being imprisoned in ice, coupled with the king's imaginative tortures, for the Highlander to forget who he'd once been. The king devoted the next two centuries to brutally training and conditioning him.

He educated the Highlander in every language spoken and instructed him in the skills, customs, and mores of each century so that he might move among mankind in any era without arousing suspicion. He trained him in every conceivable weapon and manner of fighting and endowed him with special gifts.

During the fifth and final century, the king dispatched him frequently to the mortal realm to dole out one punishment or another. Eradicating the mortal's confounded sense of honor had proven impossible, so the king utilized dark spells to compel his obedience during such missions, and if the conflict caused the mortal immeasurable pain, the king cared not. Only the end result interested the Unseelie king.

After five centuries, the man who'd once been known as Aedan MacKinnon had no recollection of his short span of thirty years in the mortal realm long ago. He no longer knew that he was mortal himself and did not understand why his king was banishing him there now.

But the king knew he owned his Vengeance only once he had fulfilled all the terms of the original agreement—the agreement the Highlander had long ago forgotten. In accordance with that agreement, the king was forbidden to coerce him with magic or instruction of any kind: Vengeance was to have his month at Dun Haakon, free of the king's meddling.

Still, the king could offer a few suggestions . . . suggestions he knew his well-trained Vengeance would construe as direct orders. After informing Vengeance—to whom time had little meaning—that the year was 1428, refreshing his knowledge of the proper customs of the century, and giving him a weighty pouch of gold coin, the Unseelie king "suggested," choosing his words carefully:

"Your body will have needs in the mortal realm. You must eat, but I would suggest you seek only bland foods."

"As you will it, my liege," Vengeance replied.

"The village of Kyleakin is near the castle wherein you'll reside. It might be best that you go there only to procure supplies and not dally therein."

"As you will it, my liege."

"Above all else, it would be unwise to seek the company of female humans or permit them to touch you."

"As you will it, my liege." A weighty pause, then, "Must I leave you?"

"It is for but a short time, my Vengeance."

Vengeance took a final look at the land he found so beautiful. "As you will it, my liege," he said.

Jane studied the tapestry, running her fingers over it, touching his face, wondering why she'd never thought to try to create a likeness of him before. What a joy it was to gaze upon him in her waking hours! She wondered where it had come from, why it had been delivered to her, if it meant he *really* existed out there somewhere. Perhaps, she decided, he'd lived long ago, and this tapestry had been his portrait, handed down from generation to generation. It looked as if it had been lovingly cared for over the centuries.

Still, that didn't explain how or why it had been sent

to *her*. She'd never told anyone about the strange recurring dreams of her Highlander. There was no logical explanation for the tapestry's arrival. Baffled, she shook her head, scattering the troubling questions from her mind, and gazed longingly at his likeness.

Funny, she mused, she'd been dreaming about him for forever, but until now she had never known his last name. He'd been only Aedan and she only Jane.

Their dream nights had been void of small talk. Theirs had been a wordless love—the quietly joyous joining of two halves of a whole. No need for questions, only for the dancing and the loving and, one day not too far off, babies. Their love transcended the need for language. The language of the heart was unmistakable.

Aedan MacKinnon. She rolled the name over and over in her mind.

She wondered and wished and ached for him, until at last, she rested her cheek against his face, curled up, and tenderly kissed his likeness. As she drifted into dreams— in that peculiar moment preceding deep sleep that always felt to Jane like falling—she thought she heard a silvery voice softly singing. The words chimed clearly, echoing in her mind:

Free him from his ice-borne hell
And in his century you both may dwell.
In the Dreaming hast thou loved him
Now, in the Waking must thou save him.

And then she thought no more, swept away on a tide of dreams.

Three

When Jane awakened there was a kitten draped across her neck, napping. Paws buried in her curly hair, it kneaded and purred deliriously, its tiny body thrumming with pleasure.

She blinked, trying to wake up. *Had there been a kitten in the box, too?* she wondered, petting its silky belly, feeling terribly guilty for failing to notice it earlier. How had it breathed in the box? Poor thing must be starved! She thought she might have some tuna in the pantry to give the little tyke. Stretching gingerly, she lifted the tiny creature off her neck and rolled over onto her side.

And shrieked.

"L-l-*lake!*" she sputtered. "There's a lake in my bedroom!" Three feet away from her. Deep blue and gently lapping at the shore. The shore that she'd been sleeping on.

Stunned, she sat up, performing a frantic mental check. Bedroom, gone. Apartment, gone. Tapestry, gone. Kitten, here. Nightie—

Gone.

"I am *so* not in the mood for an inadequacy dream," Jane hissed.

Purple flowery stuff. Here. Castle. Here.

Castle?

She rubbed her eyes with the heels of her palms. The kitten mewed and gave her an insistent head-butt, demanding more belly rubbing. She clutched the tiger-striped kitten and gaped at the castle. It looked very much like the castle she visited in her dreams, except this castle was in near ruin; a mere quarter of it stood undamaged.

"I'm still sleeping," she whispered. "I'm just dreaming that I woke up, right?" She would have been only mildly surprised had the kitten bared pearly teeth and cheekily replied.

But it didn't, so, cradling its tiny body, she rose and started walking toward the castle, wincing as her bare feet padded across stones. She tried to imagine herself some dream clothes and shoes, but it didn't work. *So much for controlling one's subconscious,* she thought. As she gazed at the portion of the castle still intact—a square central tower abutted by one wing that sported a smaller round tower—her gaze was caught by a dark flutter atop the walls. As she watched, the flutter became a shirt, the shirt a shoulder, the shoulder a man.

Her man.

She stood motionless, gazing up.

Vengeance could not fathom what had driven him to climb to the top of the tower. He'd intended to sit in the hall of the strange castle, eating only enough to survive, gazing at nothing, waiting to return to his king, but moments ago he'd felt an overwhelming compulsion to go outside. Being outside, however, was disconcerting—no cool shadows and ice but riotous color and heat—so he'd climbed instead to the walk atop the tower, where he felt less besieged by the foreign landscape.

And there she stood—the lass.

Bare as she'd been fashioned.

Something low in his gut twisted. Mayhap the cold, hard bread he'd eaten, he decided.

Distantly, he acknowledged her beauty. Flames of curly red hair framed a delicate porcelain face, tumbled down her back, and fell in ringlets over her breasts . . . breasts full and high and pink-tipped.

Legs of alabaster and rose; slender of ankle, generous of thigh. More shimmering red curls where they met. For a moment, he suffered an inexplicable inability to draw his gaze higher.

But only for a moment.

She clutched a tiny kitten to her breasts, and he had another strange moment, considering the wee beastie's lush perch, assailed by a vague and distant recollection.

It eluded him.

Unseelie females were icy creatures, with thin limbs and chill bodies.

Yet this woman didn't look icy. Nor slim. But full and generously rounded and soft and . . . warm.

It would be unwise to seek out the company of female humans or permit them to touch you, his king had ordered.

Vengeance turned his back and left the tower walk.

Jane's mouth opened and shut a dozen times while he stood at the top of the tower gazing down at her. He'd disappeared without a word. As if he didn't even know her! As if they hadn't been dream lovers for nearly forever!

As if she wasn't even standing there in all her glory, which—if one believed the love words he'd whispered in her dreams—was considerable.

Well, Jane Sillee thought irritably, *if he thinks this is a dream breakup, he's got another thought coming.*

Four

It was a little difficult to convincingly stomp into a castle nude, even in a dream.

One fretted about things like cellulite and what one's bare foot might stomp upon.

So Jane succeeded only, despite her righteous ire, in slinking into the castle, looking rather uncertain and, if her nipples were a weathervane, noticeably chilled.

He was sitting before the empty hearth, staring into it. She gazed at the fireplace wistfully, longing for a fire. It might be summer outside, but it was cold within the damp stone walls. Ever chivalrous in her dreams, he would surely accommodate her slightest wish and build a fire.

It occurred to her then that she'd never been cold in one of her dreams before. She filed the thought away for future consideration. There was something very odd about this dream.

"Aedan," she said softly.

He didn't move a muscle.

"Aedan, my love," she tried again. Perhaps he was in a bad mood, she thought, perplexed, although he'd never been in a bad mood in any of her dreams before, but she supposed there was a first time for everything. Was he angry at her for something? Had she popped in after committing some dream transgression?

He still didn't move or respond.

"Excuse me," she said not so sweetly, circling around in front of him, using the love-starved kitten as a shawl of sorts, feeling suddenly insecure, wondering what to cover, her breasts or her . . . Well, maybe he wouldn't look down.

He looked down.

When she lowered the mewing kitten, he looked up.

"That's not fair," she said, blushing. "Lend me your shirt." This was not unfolding like one of her dreams at all. Ordinarily, she didn't mind being nude with him because they were either making love in bed, or in a pile of freshly mown hay, or in a sweet, clear loch, or on a convenient table, but now he was fully clothed, and something was way off-kilter. "Please." She extended her hand.

When he shrugged, stood up, and began unlacing his linen shirt, her breath caught in her throat. When he raised one arm over his head, grabbed the nape of his shirt in a fist, and tugged it over his head, she swallowed hard. "Oh, *Aedan*," she breathed. Gorgeous. He was simply flawless, with supple muscles rippling in his arms, his chest, and his taut abdomen. She'd kissed every smooth ripple in her dreams. The sheer, visceral beauty of her Highlander hit her like a fist in the stomach, making her knees weak.

"I know not why you persist in addressing me by that appellation. I am Vengeance," he said, his voice like a blade against rough stone.

Jane's mouth popped open in an "O" of surprise. "Vengeance?" she echoed blankly, round-eyed. Then, "This *is* a dream, isn't it, Aedan?" It was quite different from her usual dream. In her dreams everything was soft-focus and fuzzed around the edges, but now things were crystal clear.

A little too clear, she thought, frowning as she glanced around.

The interior of the castle was an absolute mess. Grime and soot stained the few furnishings, and cobwebs swayed from the rafters. There was no glass in the windows, no draperies, no sumptuous tapestries, no luxurious rugs. A lone rickety chair perched before a dilapidated table that tilted lopsidedly before an empty hearth. No candles, no oil globes. It was spartan, gloomy, and downright chilly.

He pondered her question a moment. "I doona know what dreams are." There was only existing as he had always known it. Shadows and ice and his king. And pain sometimes, pain beyond fathoming. He'd learned to avoid it at all cost. "But I am not who you think."

Jane inhaled sharply, hurt and bewildered. Why was he denying who he was? It was him . . . yet not him. She narrowed her eyes, studying him. Sleek dark fall of hair—same as in her dreams. Chiseled face and sculpted jaw—same. Brilliant eyes, the color of tropical surf—not the same. Frost seemed to glitter in their depths. His sensual lips were brushed with a hint of blueness, as if from exposure to extreme cold. Everything about him seemed chilled; indeed, he might have been carved from ice and painted flesh tones.

"Yes, you are," she said firmly. "You're Aedan MacKinnon."

An odd light flashed deep within his aquamarine eyes but was as quickly gone. "Cease with that ridiculous name. I am Vengeance," he said, his deep voice ringing hollowly in the stone hall. He thrust his shirt at her.

Eagerly, she reached for it, intensely unsettled, needing clothing, some kind of armor to deflect his icy gaze. As her hand brushed his, he snatched his back, and the shirt dropped to the floor.

Doubly hurt, she stared at him a long moment, then

stooped and placed the kitten on the floor, where it promptly twined about her ankles, purring. Fumbling in her haste, she swiftly slipped the shirt over her head and tugged it down as far as it would go. The soft fabric came nearly to her knees when she rose again. The neck opening dropped to her belly button. She laced it quickly, but it did little to cover her breasts.

His gaze seemed quite fixed there.

Taking a quick deep breath, she skirted the amorous kitten and stepped toward him.

Instantly, he raised a hand. "Stay. Doona approach me. You must leave."

"Aedan, don't you know me at all?" she asked plaintively.

"Verily, I've ne'er seen you before, human. This is my place. Begone."

Jane's eyes grew huge. "Human?" she echoed. "Begone?" she snapped. "And go where? I don't know *how* to leave. I don't know how I got here. Hell's bells, I'm not certain I really *am* here or even where here is!"

"If you won't leave, I will." He rose and left the hall, slipping into the shadows of the adjoining wing.

Jane stared blankly at the space where he'd been.

Jane studied the lake a long moment before dipping her finger in, then licking it. The tiger-striped kitten sat back on its haunches, twitching its wide fluffy tail and watching her curiously.

Salt. It was no lake she was surrounded by, but the sea. *What sea?* What sea abutted Scotland? She'd never been good with geography; she was lucky she could find her way home every day. But then again, she mused, never before in one of her dreams had she bothered to wonder about geography—more evidence that this dream was strikingly abnormal.

Jane dropped down cross-legged on the rocky shore,

shaking her head. Either she'd gone completely nuts, or she was having her first-ever nightmare about her dream lover.

As she sat, rubbing her forehead and thinking hard, the soft syllables of a rhyme teased her memory. Something about saving him . . . about being in his century.

Jane Sillee, you've finally done it, she chided herself, *you've read one too many romance novels.* Only in books did heroines get swept back in time, and then they usually ended up in medieval—*oh!*

Lurching to her feet, she spun back toward the castle and took a long, hard look at her surroundings. To the left of the castle, some half-mile in the distance, was a village of thatch-roofed, wattle, and daub huts, with tendrils of smoke curling lazily skyward.

A very medieval-looking village.

She pinched herself, hard. "Ow!" It hurt. She wondered if that proved anything. "It's not possible," she assured herself. "I *must* be dreaming."

Free him from his ice-borne hell and in his century you both may dwell. In the Dreaming hast thou loved him now, in the Waking must thou save him. The rhyme, elusive a few moments ago, now resurfaced clearly in her mind.

"Impossible," she scoffed.

But what if it isn't? a small voice in her heart queried hopefully. What if the mysterious tapestry had somehow sent her back to medieval times? Accompanied by pretty clear instructions: that if she could save him, she could stay with him. In *his* century.

What century was that?

Jane snorted and shook her head.

Still, that small voice persisted with persuasive logic, *there are only three possibilities: You're dreaming. You're crazy. Or you're truly here. If you're dreaming, nothing counts, so you may as well plunge right in. If you're crazy, well, nothing counts either, so you may as*

well plunge right in. If you're really here, and you're
supposed to save him, everything counts, so you'd better
hurry up and plunge right in.

"I'm crazy," she muttered aloud. "Time-travel, my ass."

But the small voice had a point. What did she have to
lose by temporarily suspending disbelief and interacting
with her surroundings? Only by immersing herself in her
current situation might she be able to make any sense of
it. And if it were a dream, eventually she'd wake up.

But heavens, she thought, inspecting the landscape, it
all seemed so *real*. Far more real than any of her dreams
had ever been. The dainty purple bell-shaped flowers ex-
uded a sweet fragrance. The wind carried the tang of salt
from the sea. When she stooped to pet the kitten, it felt
soft and silky and had a wet little nose. If she was dreaming, it was the most detailed, incredible dream she'd ever
had.

Which made her wonder how detailed and incredible
making love with Aedan in this "dream" might be. That
was incentive enough right there to plunge in.

Her stomach growled insistently, yet another thing that
had never happened in one of her dreams. Resolutely, she
turned back toward the castle. The kitten bounded along
beside her, swiping at the occasional butterfly with gleeful
little paws, then scurrying to catch up with her again.

She would keep an open mind, she resolved as she
stepped inside the great hall. She would question him, find
out what year it supposedly was, and where she supposedly was. Then she would try to discover why he didn't
know her and why he thought he was "Vengeance."

Aedan sat again, as he had before, staring into the
empty fireplace. Clad in loose black trousers, boots, and
a gloriously naked upper torso, he was as still as death.

When she perched on the chilly stone hearth before
him, his eyes glittered dangerously. "I thought you left,"
he growled.

"I told you, I don't know how to leave," she said simply.

Vengeance considered her words. Had his king deliberately placed the female human there? If so, why? Always before when his king had sent him into the mortal realm, Vengeance had been given precise instructions, a specific mission to accomplish. But not this time. He knew not what war to cause, whose ear to poison with lies, or whom to maim or kill. Mayhap, he brooded, this was his king's way of testing him, of seeing if Vengeance could determine what his king wanted of him.

He studied her. There was no denying it, he was curious about the human. She was the antithesis of all he'd encountered in his life; vibrant, with her flaming hair and curvy body. Pale porcelain skin and rosy lips. Eyes of molten amber fringed by dusky lashes and slanted upward at the outer corners. She had many facial expressions, lively muscles that pulled her lips up and down and many which ways. He found himself wondering what she would feel like, were he to touch her, if she was as soft and warm as she looked.

"Would you mind building me a fire?" she asked.

"I am not cold. Nor do you look cold," he added, his gaze raking over her. She looked far warmer than aught he'd seen.

"Well, I am. Fire. Now, please," she said firmly.

After a moment's hesitation, he complied with her command, layering the bricks, making swift work of it, never taking his gaze from her. He felt greatly intrigued by her breasts. He could not fathom what it was about those soft plump mounds beneath the worn linen that so commanded his attention. Were they on his own body, he would have been appalled by the excess fatty flesh, yet gazing upon her, he found his fingers clenching and unclenching, desirous to touch, perhaps cup their plump weight in his hands. For a mere human, she had a powerful presence. He considered the possibility that—wee as she was—she might be quite dangerous. After all, there were things in Faery minute of stature capable of inflicting unspeakable pain.

"Thank you," she said, rubbing her hands together before the blaze that sputtered in the hearth. "Those are peat bricks, aren't they? I read about them once."

"Aye."

"Interesting," she murmured thoughtfully. "They don't look like I thought they did." Then she shook her head sharply and focused on him again. "What is the name of this castle?"

"Dun Haakon," he replied, then started. Where had that name come from? His king had told him naught about his temporary quarters.

"Where am I?"

More knowledge he had no answers for: "On *Eilean A Cheo.*"

"Where?" she asked blankly.

" 'Tis Gaelic for 'misty isle.' We are on the Isle of Skye." Mayhap it was knowledge his king had taught him long ago, he decided. There, silent until needed. His king had oft told him he'd prepared him for any place, any time.

Jane took a deep breath. "What year is it?"

"Fourteen hundred twenty-eight."

She inhaled sharply. "And how long have you lived here?"

"I doona live here. I am to remain but one passing of the moon. I arrived yestreen."

"Where *do* you live?"

"You have many questions." He reflected for a moment, and decided there was no harm in answering her questions. He was, after all, Vengeance. Powerful. Perfect. Deadly. "I live with my king in his kingdom."

"And where is that?"

"In Faery."

Jane swallowed. "Fairy?" she said weakly.

"Aye. My king is the Unseelie king. I am his Vengeance. And I am perfect," he added, as if an afterthought.

"That's highly debatable," Jane muttered.

"Nay. 'Tis not. I am perfect. My king tells me so. He tells me I will be the most feared warrior ever to live, that the name of Vengeance will endure in legend for eternity."

"I'm quaking," Jane said dryly, with an aggrieved expression.

He looked at her then, hard. Her hair, her face, her breasts, then lower still, his gaze lingering on her smooth bare legs and slender ankles. "You are not at all what I expected of humans," he said finally.

Go with it, she told herself. *Since none of this makes any sense, just run with what he's told you and see where it leads.* "You aren't what I expected of a fairy," she said lightly. "Aren't you supposed to have sparkly little wings?"

"I doona think I am a fairy," he said carefully.

"Then you're human?" she pressed.

He looked perplexed, then gave a faint shake of his head.

"Well, if you're not a fairy and you're not human, what are you?"

His brows dipped and he shifted uncomfortably but made no reply.

"Well?" she encouraged.

After a long pause he said, "I will be needing my shirt back, lass. You may find clothing in the round tower down the corridor." He pointed behind her. "Go now."

"We're not done with this conversation, Aedan," she said, eyes narrowing.

"Vengeance."

"I'm not going to stop asking questions, *Aedan.* I have oodles of them."

He shrugged, rose, and wandered over to the window, turning his back to her.

"And I'm hungry, and when I get hungry I get grumpy. You do have food, don't you?"

He remained stoically silent. A few moments later he heard her snort, then stomp off in search of clothing.

If you're not a fairy and you're not human, what are you? Her question hung in the air after she'd left, unanswered. Unanswerable.

Verily, he didn't know.

Five

She was a demanding creature.

Vengeance ended up having to make three trips into Kyleakin to acquire those things the lass deemed "the bare necessities." It was abundantly clear that she had no plans of leaving. Indeed, she intended to loll in the lap of luxury for the duration of her stay. Because he wasn't certain if his liege had arranged her presence as part of some mysterious plan he'd chosen not to impart, and because he'd been told to reside at the castle until summoned, it seemed he must share his temporary quarters. He was greatly uneasy and just wished he knew what was expected of him. How could he act on his king's behalf if he knew not why he was there?

On his first foray into Kyleakin—the only trip made of his own volition while she'd been occupied rummaging through trunks in the round tower—he'd purchased naught but day-old bread so they both might eat that eve. Although he found the heat and colors of the landscape chafing, he was relieved to escape her disconcerting presence and foolishly believed procuring food might silence her ever-wagging tongue.

When she discovered he'd "gone shopping" without informing her, she'd tossed her mass of shining curls and scowled, ordering him to procure additional items. The second time he'd spent a fair amount of the gold coin his liege had given him purchasing clean (so mayhap they were a bit scratchy and rough, but *he* didn't even need them to begin with) woolens, meat, cheese, fruit, quills, ink, and three fat, outrageously costly sheets of parchment—the parchment and quills because she'd proclaimed she was "a writer" and it was imperative she write every day without fail. At first he'd been puzzled by her bragging that she knew her letters, then he realized it was, like as not, a rare achievement for a mere mortal. He imagined he knew many more letters than she, and if she still needed to practice them, she was a sorry apprentice indeed.

Unimpressed with the results of his second expedition, she'd sent him back a *third* time, with a tidy little list on a scrap of parchment, to find more parchment, coffee beans or strong tea, a cauldron, mugs, eating tools, a supply of rags and vinegar for cleaning, *soft* woolens, down ticks, wine, and "unless you wish to fish the sea yourself," fresh fish for the useless furry beastie.

Vengeance, being ordered about by a wee woman. Fetching food for a mouse-catcher.

Still, she was a mesmerizing thing. Especially in the pale pink gown she'd dug out of one of the many trunks. Her eyes sparkled with irritation or as she listed her demands, her breasts jiggled softly when she gestured, then she turned all cooing and tender as she stooped to scratch the beastie behind its furry ears.

Making him wonder what her slender fingers might feel like in his hair.

He was unprepared for one such as she and wondered

why his king had not forewarned him that humans could be so . . . intriguing. None that he'd e'er encountered in his past travels had been so compelling, and his king had e'er painted them as coarse, sullen, and stupid creatures, easily manipulated by higher beings like Vengeance.

He'd not yet manipulated the smallest portion of his current circumstances, too busy being ordered about by her. *Build me a fire, give me your shirt, buy me this, buy me that. Hmph!* What might she demand next? He—the formidable hand of the fairy king's wrath—was almost afraid to find out.

"Kiss me."

"What?" he said blankly.

"Kiss me," she repeated, with an encouraging little nod.

Vengeance stepped back, inwardly cursing himself for retreating, but something about the fiery lass made him itch to flee to the farthest reaches of the isle. At her direction, he'd fluffed several heavy down ticks on the sole bed in the keep. She was happily spreading it with soft woolens and a luxurious green velvet throw he'd not intended to buy. He'd been coerced into taking it by the proprietor, who'd been delighted to hear a woman was in residence at Dun Haakon and had eagerly inquired "Be ye the new laird and lady of Dun Haakon?" Scowling, he'd flung coin at the shopkeeper, snatched up the bed-clothes, and made haste from the establishment.

He was beginning to resent that his king had given him no orders. There, in his dark kingdom, Vengeance knew who he was and what his aim. Here, he was lost, abandoned in a stifling, garish world he did not understand, surrounded by creatures he could not fathom, with not one word of guidance from his liege.

And now the wench wanted him to do something else. Precisely what, he wasn't certain, but he suspected it boded ill for him. She was a creature greatly preoccupied with her physical comforts, and down that path—so his king oft said—lay weakness, folly, and ruin. Vengeance had few physical needs, merely food, water, and the occasional hour of rest.

"Kiss me," she said, making a plump pucker with her lips. She gave the velvet coverlet a final smoothing. "I think it might help you remember."

"What exactly is a kiss?" he asked suspiciously.

Her eyes widened and she regarded him with amazement. "You don't know what a kiss is?" she exclaimed.

"Why should I? 'Tis a mortal thing, is it not?"

She cocked her head and looked as if she were having a heated internal debate. After a moment she appeared to reach a decision and stepped closer to him. Stoically, he held his ground this time, refusing to cede an inch.

"I merely want to press my lips against yours," she said, innocence knitted to a disarming smile. "Push them together, like so." She demonstrated, and the lush moue of her mouth tugged something deep in his groin.

"Nay. You may not touch me," he said stiffly.

She leaned closer. He caught a faint scent, something sweet and flowery on her fiery tresses. It made him want to press his face to her hair, inhale greedily, and stroke the coppery curls.

He leaned back. Fortunately, the lass was too short to reach his face without his cooperation. Or a step stool.

"You are so stubborn," she said, with a gusty sigh. "Fine, let's talk then. It's pretty clear we have a *lot* to talk about." She paused, then, "He doesn't know what kisses are," she muttered to herself, shaking her head. "*That's* never happened in my dreams before." Perching on the end of the bed, her feet dangling, she patted the space beside her. "Come. Sit by me."

"Nay." When the kitten jumped daintily onto the bed and spilled across the velvet coverlet, he scowled at it. "You or that bedraggled mop of fur—I'm fair uncertain which is more useless. At least the beastie doesna prattle on so."

"But the beastie can't kiss either," she said archly. "And it's not bedraggled. Don't insult my kitten," she added defensively.

"You attribute high value to these kisses of yours. I scarce believe they are worth much," he said scornfully.

"That's because you haven't kissed me yet. If you did, you'd know."

Vengeance moved, in spite of his best intentions, to stand at the foot of the bed between her legs. He stared down at her. She scooped up the kitten and pressed her lips to its furry head. He closed his eyes and fought a tide of images that made no sense to him.

"Perhaps you're afraid," she said sweetly.

He opened his eyes. "I fear nothing."

"Then why won't you let me do something so harmless? See? The kitten survived unscathed."

He struggled with the answer for a moment, then said simply, "You may not touch me. 'Tis forbidden."

"Why not, and by whom?"

"I obey my king. And 'tis none of your concern why."

"I think it is. I thought you were a man who thought for himself. A warrior, a leader. Now you tell me you follow orders like some little puppet."

"Puppet?"

"An imitation of a real person fashioned of wood, pulled this way and that by its master. You're nothing but a servant, are you?"

Her delicate sneer cut him to the quick, and he flinched angrily. Who was she calling a servant? He was Vengeance, he was perfect and strong and . . . *Och, he* was *his king's servant.* Why did that chafe? Why did he suffer the odd sensation that once he'd not been anyone's serf but a leader in his own right?

"Why do you obey him?" she pressed. "Does this king

of yours mean so much to you? Is he so good to you? Tell me about him."

Vengeance opened his mouth, closed it again, and left the room silently.

"Where are you going?" she called after him.

"To prepare a meal, then you will sleep and leave me in peace," he growled over his shoulder.

Jane ate in bed, alone but for the kitten. Aedan brought her fish roasted over an open fire and a blackened potato that had obviously been stuffed in the coals to cook, accompanied by a similarly charred turnip, then left in silence. No salt. No butter for the dry potato. Not one drop of lemon for the fish.

Warily, she conceded that she was probably not dreaming—the fare had never been so unpalatable in one of her dreams. And upon reflection, she realized that although she'd attended many dream feasts, she'd never actually eaten anything at any of them. Now, she choked it down because she was too emotionally drained to attempt cooking for herself over an open fire. Tomorrow was another day.

The tiger-striped kitten, whom she'd christened Sexpot (after apologetically peeking beneath her tail) because of the way the little tyke sashayed about as if outrageously pleased with herself, hungrily devoured a tender fish filet, then busied herself scrubbing her whiskers with little spit-moistened paws while Jane puzzled over her situation.

She'd been astonished to discover Aedan had no idea what a kiss was, but the more she thought about it, the more sense it made.

Aedan not only didn't know he was Aedan, he didn't remember that he was a *man,* hence he didn't recall the intimacies of lovemaking!

She wondered if that made him a virgin of sorts. When they finally made love—and there was no doubt in her mind that they would, one way or another, even if she had to ambush and attack him—would he have any idea what it was all about? How strange to think that she might have to teach him, he who'd been her inexhaustible dream tutor.

He certainly hadn't liked being provoked, she mused. He'd grown increasingly agitated when she'd mocked him for obeying his king and had visibly bristled at the idea of being a mere servant. Still, despite such promising re-actions, he had a formidable shell that was going to be difficult to penetrate. It would help if she knew what had happened to him. She needed to make him talk about his "king," and find out when and how they'd met. Were there indeed a "fairy king," perhaps the being had en-chanted him. The idea taxed Jane's credulity, but, all things considered, she supposed she couldn't suspend dis-belief without suspending it fully. Until she reached some concrete conclusions about what was going on, she would be unwise to discount any possibilities.

Whatever had happened to him, she had to undo it. She hoped it wouldn't take too long, because she wasn't sure how long she could stand watching her soulmate glare at her with blatant distrust and dislike. Withholding kisses. Refusing to let her touch him.

You have one month here with him, no more, a woman's lilting voice whispered.

Sexpot stopped grooming, paw frozen before her face. She arched into a horseshoe shape and emitted a ferocious hiss.

"Wh-what?" Jane stammered, glancing about.

Cease with your absurd protestations that this place is not real. You are *in the fifteenth century, Jane Sillee. And here you may stay, if you succeed. You have but one full cycle of the moon in the sky to make him remember who he is.*

Jane opened her mouth, closed it, and opened it again, but nothing came out. Sexpot suffered no such problem, growling low and long. Gently smoothing the spiked hairs on the kitten's back, Jane wet her lips and swallowed. "That's impossible, the man will hardly speak to me! And who are you?" she demanded. *I'm talking to a disembodied voice,* she thought, bewildered.

I'm not the one who doesn't know. Worry about him.

"Don't be cryptic. Who are you?" Jane hissed.

There was no reply. After a few moments, Sexpot's back no longer resembled a porcupine's, and Jane realized that whoever had spoken was gone.

"Well, just what am I supposed to do?" she shouted angrily. A month wasn't a whole lot of time to figure out what had happened to him and to help him remember who he was. She'd like to know who was making up the rules. She had a bone or two to pick with them.

Aedan appeared in the doorway, glancing hastily about the chamber. Only after ascertaining she was alone and in no apparent danger did he speak. "What are you yelling about?" he demanded.

Jane stared at him, framed in the doorway, gilded by a shaft of silvery moonlight that spilled in the open window, his sculpted chest bare, begging her touch.

She was suddenly stricken by two certainties that she felt in the marrow of her bones: that as the woman had said, she truly was in the fifteenth century, and that if she didn't help him remember, something terrible beyond her ability to imagine would become of him. Would he live and die the icy, inhuman creature he'd become? Perhaps turn into something even worse?

"Oh, Aedan," she said, the words hitching in her throat. All her love and longing and fear were in his name.

"I am *Vengeance*," he snarled. "When will you accept that?"

When he spun about and stalked from the chamber, Jane sat for a long time, looking around, examining everything anew, wondering how she could have thought for even a moment that she might be dreaming. The reason everything had seemed so real was because it *was* so real.

She fell back onto the bed and stared at the cobwebby ceiling through the shimmer of silent tears. "I won't lose you, Aedan," she whispered.

*Hours later, Vengeance stood at the foot of the bed, watch*ing her sleep. He'd passed a time of restless slumber on the floor in the hall and awakened intensely agitated. His rest had not been of the kind he'd known in Faery—an edgy, mostly aware state of short duration. Nay, he'd fallen into deep oblivion for far longer than usual, and his slumbering mind had gone on strange journeys. Upon awakening, his memory of those places had dissolved with the suddenness of a bubble bursting, leaving him with the nagging feeling that he'd forgotten something of import.

Troubled, he'd sought her. She was sprawled on her back, pink gown bunched about her thighs, masses of fiery curls about her face. The kitten of which she seemed strangely fond—and it was too stringy to be palatable over a fire, nor was it capable of useful labor, hence her interest in it baffled him—was also sprawled on its back and had managed to insinuate itself into her hair. Its tiny paws curled and uncurled while it emitted a most odd sound. A bit of drool escaped its thin pink lips.

Cautiously, Vengeance lowered himself onto the bed. The lass stirred and stretched but did not awaken. The kitten curled itself into a circle and purred louder.

Gingerly, Vengeance plucked up a ringlet of her hair and held it between his fingers. It shimmered in the moonlight, all the hues of flame: golden and coppery and bronze. It was unlike aught he'd seen before. There were more colors in a simple hank of her hair than had been in the entirety of his world until yesterday.

He smoothed the curl between his thumb and forefinger.

The kitten opened a golden eye and stared at Vengeance's dark hand.

It did not flee him, he mused, which confirmed he wasn't fairy; for 'twas well known that cats loathed fairies. On the other hand, it didn't attempt to touch him, which he supposed meant he wasn't human either, for the thing certainly flung itself at the lass at every opportunity.

So what am I?

Sliding his hand beneath her tresses, he sneaked a quick glance at her. Her eyes were still closed, her lips slightly parted. Her breasts rising and falling gently.

Two hands.

It felt. So. Good.

There certainly was a lot of touching going on in this place. Even the kitten seemed to crave it. And she—ah, *she* touched everything. Petted the beastie, stroked the velvety coverlet he'd procured in Kyleakin, and would have touched him a dozen times or more—he'd seen it in her eyes. *Kiss me,* she'd said, and he'd nearly crushed her in his arms, intrigued by this "pressing of the lips" she'd described. The mere thought of touching such warmth did alarming things to his body. Tentatively, he touched the tip of his index finger to her cheek, then snatched it away.

The kitten buried its pink nose in her hair. After a moment's pause, Vengeance did, too. Then rested his cheek lightly against it, absorbing the sensation against his skin.

Why do you obey him? Is he so good to you?

Vengeance tried to ponder that thought. His king was . . . well, his king. What right did Vengeance have to question whether his liege was good to him? It was not his place!

Why not? For the first time in centuries, unhampered by the constant coercion of the king's dark spells, an independent thought sprouted and thrust down a thick taproot in his mind. He had no idea whence such a blasphemous thought had come, but it had, and it defied his efforts to cast it out. Pain lanced through his head behind his eyes. Excruciating pressure built at his temples, and he clamped his hands to his ears as if to silence voices only he could hear.

Aedan, come quickly, I have something to show you. Da brought me a baby pine marten! A lass's voice, a lass who'd once been terribly important to him. A wee child of eight, about whom he'd fretted and tried to protect. *Mary, she'll be fine with the wee pet,* a man's voice said.

But we're sailin' out on the morrow, Mary protested. *'Tis wounded and might harm her without meanin' to.*

Aedan has a way with the wee creatures, and he'll watch o'er his sister.

"Aedan," he breathed, testing the sound of it on his tongue.

"Vengeance," he whispered after a moment.

Neither name fit him like skin on bones. Neither place he'd been—neither his land of ice nor this isle—felt like well-worn boots, broken in and suited to the heel.

He suffered a fierce urge to claw his way from his own body, so strange and ill-fashioned did it suddenly seem. In his king's land he knew who he was and what purpose he served. But here, och, here, he knew nothing.

Nothing but pain in places deep in his head and tingles in places deep in his groin.

Warily, he eyed the pale curves of her legs peeking from the hem of the gown. How smooth they looked . . . how warm.

He squeezed his eyes tightly shut, envisioning his beloved home with his king.

Be ye the new laird and lady of Dun Haakon? the shopkeeper queried brightly in his mind, obliterating his soothing image of ice and shadow.

"Nay," he whispered. "I am Vengeance."

Six

The villagers descended upon the castle at daybreak.

Jane awakened slowly, feeling disoriented and vulnerable. She'd not dreamed of Aedan, and if she'd suffered any remnants of doubts that she was in the fifteenth century before she'd fallen asleep, they were gone now. She'd never slept through an entire night without at least one dream of her Highland love.

At first she wasn't certain what had awakened her, then the clamor of voices rose in the hall beyond the open door of the bedchamber. High-pitched and excited, they were punctuated by stilted, grudging replies in Aedan's deep burr.

Swiftly she performed her morning ritual of positive reinforcement by announcing brightly to the empty bedchamber, "It's today! What better day could it be?" She'd read somewhere that such small litanies were useful in setting one's mood, so she recited it each morning without fail. Yesterday was a memory. Tomorrow was a hope.

Today was another day to live and do one's best to love. In her estimation that was pretty much all a person could ask.

Kissing the drowsy kitten on the head, she slipped from the bed, quickly stripped off her wrinkled dress, then donned the simple yellow gown she'd unearthed yesterday while going through the trunks. She was looking forward to wearing it, because it was undeniably romantic with its low, laced bodice and flowing skirt. Coupled with the complete lack of undergarments in any of the trunks, she felt positively sinful. Ready for her man at any moment. How she hoped it would be today!

Casting a quick glance about the room, she narrowed her eyes thoughtfully. She was going to want a few more items from the nearby village, and soon, specifically a large bathtub and whatever medieval people used for toothpaste and soap. Lured by the hum of voices, she hurried from the bedchamber.

*Vengeance backed against the hearth like a cornered an-*imal. A dozen yammering villagers thrust baked goods and gifts at him and prattled nonstop about some legend and how delighted they were to have a MacKinnon back to watch over them. How they would serve him faithfully. How they planned to rebuild his castle.

Him—watch over them? He'd as soon sweep his hand and raze the room, leaving naught but bones and silence!

But he kept both his hands, and the fairy gifts of destructive power his king had given him, carefully behind his back, because he didn't know what the blethering hell his liege wanted. Rage simmered in his veins—rage at the villagers, rage at his liege—stunning him with its intensity. Then *she* sauntered in and some of the rage dissipated, ousted by discomfort of another sort, slightly more palatable but no less disconcerting.

She was a sunbeam flickering about the gloomy interior

of the hall. As he watched in tense silence, she smiled and spoke and took the villagers' hands in hers, welcoming the entire ragamuffin lot of them into what had been, for a blissfully short time, *his* quarters alone. How and when had he so completely lost control of himself and his environ? he wondered. Was control something the Fates leeched away slowly over a period of time, or a thing instantaneously nihilated by the mere appearance of a female? Enter woman—exit order.

And och, how they were smiling at her, beaming and adoring, clearly accepting her as their lady!

"She's *not* a MacKinnon," he snapped. Best he swiftly disabuse them of the foolish notion that he was laird and she lady.

All heads swiveled to look at him.

"Milord," one of them said hesitantly after a pained pause, " 'tis naught of our concern if ye've handfasted her or no. We're simply pleased to welcome ye both."

"Nor am *I* a MacKinnon," he said stiffly.

A dozen people gaped, then burst into uneasy laughter. An elderly man with silver hair, clad in russet trews and a linen shirt, shook his head and smiled gently. "Come," he beckoned, hastening from the hall into the adjoining wing.

Wholly irritated with himself for doing so, Vengeance sought the lass's gaze. He was so accustomed to obeying orders that making simple decisions, like whether or not to follow the elder, paralyzed him. He despised the confusion he felt, despised being left to his own devices. She stepped toward him, looking as if she planned to tuck her hand through his arm. Baring his teeth in a silent snarl, he spun around and followed the old man. Better his own decisions, he decided, then to rely upon *her*.

A few moments later, he stood in the round tower watching the elderly man remove dusty woolens draped over objects stacked behind an assortment of trunks near the wall. The elder seemed to be looking for one item in particular, and upon locating it, devoted much care to wiping it free of dust. Then he swiveled it about and propped it in front of him, where all could see.

Vengeance sucked in a harsh breath. The elder had uncovered a portrait of a dark-haired girl sitting between a man and a woman. The man bore an eerie resemblance to himself. The woman was a beauty with wild blond tresses. But the little girl—ah, merely gazing upon her filled him with pain. He closed his eyes, his breathing suddenly rapid and shallow.

But you canna leave me, Aedan! Ma and Da hae gone sailin' and I canna bear to be alone! Nay, Aedan, dinna be leavin' me! I've a terrible feelin' you willna be comin' back!

But this "Aedan," whoever he was, had had to leave. He'd had no choice.

Vengeance wondered who the man and child were and how he knew of them. But such thoughts pained his head so he thrust them from his mind. 'Twas none of his concern.

" 'Tis Findanus and Saucy Mary, with their daughter, Rose," the old man informed him. "They promised centuries ago that although the keep might be abandoned, one day a MacKinnon would return, the village would prosper, and the castle would be filled with clan again."

"I am *not* a MacKinnon," Vengeance growled.

The elder retrieved yet another portrait of three men riding into battle. Even Vengeance was forced to concede his resemblance to them was startling.

" 'Tis Duncan, Robert, and Niles MacKinnon. The brothers were killed fighting for Robert the Bruce more than a century ago. The keep has stood vacant since. The remaining MacKinnon resettled easterly, on the mainland."

"I am no kin of theirs," Vengeance said stiffly.

The lass who'd invaded his castle snorted. "You look

just like them. Anyone can see the resemblance. You're obviously a MacKinnon."

" 'Tis an uncanny coincidence, naught more."

The villagers were silent for a time, watching their elder for a cue. The old man measured him for several moments, then spoke in a tone one might employ to gentle a wild animal. "We came to offer our services. We brought food, drink, and materials to rebuild. We will arrive each morn at daybreak and remain as yer servants 'til dusk. We pray ye choose to remain with us. 'Tis clear ye are a warrior and a leader. Whatever name ye go by, we would be pleased to call ye laird."

Vengeance felt a peculiar helplessness steal over him. The man was saying that whether he was MacKinnon or not, they needed a protector and they wanted *him*. He felt a simultaneous disdain, a sense that he was above it all, yet . . . a tentative tide of pleasure.

He longed to put a stop to it—to cast the villagers out, to force the female to leave—but not being privy to his king's purpose in sending him there, he couldn't, lest he undermine his liege's plan. It was possible that his king expected him to submit to a fortnight of mortal doings to prove how stoically he could endure and demonstrate how well he would perform amongst them in the future. There was also the possibility that since he was his king's emissary in the mortal realm, he might have future need of this castle, and his king *intended* the villagers to rebuild it. He shook his head, unable to fathom why he'd been abandoned without direction.

"Oh, how lovely of you to offer!" the lass exclaimed. "How kind you all are! We'd *love* your help. I'm Jane, by the way," she told the elder, clasping his hand and smiling. "Jane Sillee."

Vengeance left the tower without saying another word. *Jane*. He rolled the name over in his mind. She was called Jane. "Jane Sillee," he whispered. He liked the sound of it on his lips.

His head began to pound again.

*   *   *

"What's ailing him, milady?" Elias, the village elder, asked after Aedan had departed and introductions had been made all around.

"He suffered a fall and took a severe blow to his head," she lied smoothly. "It may be some time before he's himself again. His memory has suffered, and he's uncertain of many things."

"Is he a MacKinnon from one o' their holdings in the east?" Elias asked.

Jane nodded, ruing the lie but deeming it necessary.

"I was fair certain, there's no mistakin' the look," Elias said. "Since the battle at Bannockburn, they've left the isle untended, busy with their holdings on the mainland. Long have we prayed they would send one of their kin to stand for us, to reside on the isle again."

"And so they have, but he was injured on the way here and we must help him remember," Jane said, seizing the opportunity offered, grateful that she now had co-conspirators. "Touch him frequently, although it may appear to unsettle him," she told them. "I believe it helps. And bring children around," she said, remembering how in her dreams Aedan had adored children. "The more the better. Perhaps they could play in the yard while we work."

"We? *Ye* needn't labor like a serf, milady," a young woman exclaimed.

"I intend to be part of rebuilding our home," Jane said firmly. *Our home*—how she liked the sound of that! She was gratified to see a glint of appreciation in the women's eyes. There were several approving nods.

"Also, I heard somewhere that familiar scents can help stir memories, so if you wouldn't mind teaching me to bake some things you think he might like, I'd be most appreciative. I'm afraid I'm not the best cook," she admitted. "But I'm eager to learn."

More approving nods.

Jane beamed. Her morning litany really did help: Today was turning out to be a fine day after all.

Seven

And so they settled into a routine with which Jane was pleased, despite Aedan's continued insistence that he was not a MacKinnon. Days sped by, too quickly for Jane's liking, but small progress was being made both with the estate and with the taciturn, brooding man who called himself Vengeance. Each day, Jane felt more at home at Dun Haakon, more at home with being in the fifteenth century.

As promised, each morning at daybreak, the villagers arrived in force. They were hard workers, and although the men departed in the late afternoon to tend their own small plots of land, the women and children remained, laboring cheerfully at Jane's side. They swept and scrubbed the floors; scraped away cobwebs; polished old earthenware mugs and platters, candlesticks, and oil globes; and aired out tapestries, hanging them with care. They repaired and oiled what furniture remained, stored beneath cloths saturated with the dust of decades.

Before long, the great hall sported a gleaming honey-blond table and a dozen chairs. The sole bed had been lavishly (and with much giggling by the women) covered with the plumpest pillows and softest fabrics the village had to offer. Sconces were reattached to the stone walls, displaying sparkling globes of oil with fat, waxy wicks. The women stitched pillows for the wooden chairs and strung packets of herbs from the beams.

The kitchen had fallen into complete rubble decades ago, and it would take some time to rebuild. After much thought, Jane decided it wasn't *too* risky to suggest the piping of water from a freshwater spring behind the castle and direct the construction of a large reservoir over a four-sided hearth, guaranteeing hot water at a moment's notice. She also sketched plans for counters and cabinets and a massive centrally located butcher's block.

In the meantime, Jane was learning to cook over the open fire in the great hall. Each afternoon the women taught her a new dish. Unfortunately, each evening, she ate it with a man who refused to eat anything but hard bread, no matter how she tried to tempt him.

Late into the twilight hours, Jane scribbled busily away before the fire, sometimes making notes, sometimes working on her manuscript, all the while peeking at Aedan over her papers and writing the future she hoped to have with him. She liked the laborious ritual of using quill and ink, the flames in the open hearth licking at her slippered toes, the hum of crickets and soft hooting of owls. She relished the complete absence of tires screeching, car alarms pealing, and planes flying overhead. In all her life, she'd never experienced such absolute, awe-inspiring stillness.

By the end of the first week of renovations, she'd begun to draw hope from Aedan's bewildered silence. Although he refused to speak to her, day by day, he participated a bit more in the repairs to the estate. And day by day, he seemed a bit less forbidding. No longer did she see disdain and loathing in his gaze, but confusion and . . . un-

certainty? As if he didn't understand his place and how
he fit into the grand scheme of things.

Jane intended to use her month as wisely as possible.
She learned in her psychology courses at Purdue that at-
tacking "amnesia" head-on could drive the person deeper
into denial, even induce catatonia. So after much hard
thought, she'd decided to give Aedan two weeks of absolutely no pressure, other than acclimating to his new
environment. Two weeks of working, of being silently
companionable, of not touching him as she so longed to
do, despite the misery of being with him but forbidden to
demonstrate her love and affection.

After those two weeks, she promised herself the seduc-
tion would begin. No more baths in Kyleakin in one of
the village women's homes. She would begin bathing before the fire in the hall. No more proper gowns in the
evening. She would wear lower bodices and higher hems.

And so, Jane bided her time, cuddled with Sexpot in
the luxurious bed, and dreamed about the night when Aedan would lay beside her and speak her name in those
husky tones that promised lovemaking to make a girl's
toes curl.

Aedan stood on the recently repaired front steps of the
castle and stretched his arms above his head, easing the
tightness in his back. The night sky was streaked with
purple. Stars twinkled above the treetops, and a crescent
moon silvered the lawn. Every muscle in his body was
sore from toting heavy stones from a nearby quarry to the
castle.

Although he'd learned to avoid pain in the land of shadows, the current aches in his body were a strangely plea-
surable sensation. He'd refused to participate in the repairs
at first, withholding himself in silent and aloof censure,
but much to his surprise, as he'd watched the village men
work, he'd begun to hanker to lift, carry, and patch. His

hands had itched to get dirty, and his mind had been eager to redesign parts of the keep that had been inefficiently, and in places, hazardously constructed.

Pondering the three commands his king had given, he'd concluded there was nothing to prevent him from passing time more quickly by working.

When on the third day he'd silently joined the men, they'd worked with twice the vigor and smiled and jested more frequently. They asked his opinion on many things, leading him to discover with some surprise that he *had* opinions, and, further, that they seemed sound. They accepted him with minimal fuss, although they touched him with disconcerting frequency, clapping him on the shoulder and patting his arm.

Because they weren't females, he deemed it acceptable.

When they asked the occasional question, he evaded. He completely ignored the lass who doggedly remained in the castle, leaving only to traipse off to the village, from whence she returned clean and slightly damp.

And fragrant smelling. And warm and soft and sweet looking.

Sometimes, merely gazing upon her made him hurt inside.

Vengeance shook his head, as if to shake thoughts of her right out of it. With each passing day, things seemed different. The sky no longer seemed too brilliant to behold, the air no longer too stifling to breathe. He'd begun to anticipate working each day, because in the gloaming he could stand back and look at something—a wall recently shored up, steps re-laid, a roof repaired, an interior hearth redesigned—and know it was his doing. He liked the feeling of laboring and rued that his king might deem it a flaw in his character, unsuitable for an exalted being.

And each day, when his thoughts turned toward his king, they were more often than not resentful thoughts. His king might not have bothered to inform him of his purpose at Dun Haakon, but the humans were more than willing to offer him ample purpose.

Purpose without pain.

Without *any* pain at all.

He had a blasphemous thought that took him by surprise and caused a headache of epic proportions that throbbed all through the night: He wondered if mayhap his king mightn't just forget about him.

Eight

Swiftly did one blasphemous thought breed another, the next more blasphemous, making the prior seem nearly innocuous. Swiftly did traitorous thought manifest itself in traitorous action.

It was on the evening of the eleventh day of his exile, when she was laying her meal on the long table in the great hall, that Vengeance began his fall from grace.

He'd labored arduously that day, and more than once his grip had slipped on a heavy stone. Furthering his unease, wee children from the village had played on the front lawn all afternoon. The sound of their high voices, bubbling with laughter as they chased a bladder-ball at the edge of the surf or teased the furry beastie with woolen yarns, had reverberated painfully inside his skull.

Now, he sat in the corner, far from the hearth, chewing dispiritedly on hard bread. Of late, he'd been eating loaf after loaf of it, his body starved by his daily labors. Yet no matter how much bread he consumed, he continued to lose mass and muscle and to feel lethargic and weak. He knew 'twas why his grip had slipped today.

Of late, when she spread the table with her rich and savory foods, his stomach roiled angrily, and on previous evenings, he'd left the castle and walked outdoors to avoid temptation.

But recently, indeed only this morning, he'd thought long and hard about his king's remark concerning sustenance and had scrutinized the precise words of his command.

You must eat, but I would suggest you seek only bland foods.

I would suggest.

It was the most nebulous phrase his liege had ever uttered. *I would suggest.* That was not at all how his king spoke to Vengeance. It made one think the king might be . . . uncertain of himself, unwilling, for some unfathomable reason, to commit to a command. And "bland." How vague was bland? An engraved invitation to interpretation, that word was.

After much meditation, Vengeance concluded for himself—a thing coming shockingly easier each day—that apparently his king had suffered some uncertainty as to how hard Vengeance might be laboring, so he'd been unable to anticipate what sustenance his body would require. Thus, he had "suggested," leaving the matter to Vengeance's discretion. As his king had placed such a trust in him, Vengeance resolved he must not return to his king weakened in body and risk inciting his displeasure.

When he rose and joined her at the table, her eyes rounded in disbelief.

"I will dine with you this eve," he informed her, gazing at her. Nay, lapping her up with his eyes. The tantalizing scent of roasted suckling pig teased his nostrils; the glorious rainbow hues of fiery-haired Jane clad in an emerald gown teased something he couldn't name.

"No bread?" she managed after an incredulous pause.

" 'Tis not enough to sustain me through the day's labors."

"I see," she said carefully, as she hastened to lay another setting.

Vengeance eyed the food with great interest. She served him generous portions of roast pork swimming in juices and glazed with a jellied sauce, roasted potatoes in clotted cream with chive, some type of vegetable mix in yet another sauce, and thin strips of battered salmon. As a finishing touch, she added several ladles of a buttery-looking pudding.

When she placed it before him, he continued to eye it, knowing he'd not yet gone too far. He could still rise and return to his corner, to his bread.

I would suggest.

He glanced at her. She had a spoon in her mouth and was licking the clotted cream from it. That was all it took. He fell upon the food like a ravening beast, eating with his bare hands, shoving juicy, deliciously greasy pork into his mouth, stripping the tender meat from the bones with his teeth and tongue.

Christ, it was heavenly! Rich and succulent and warm.

Jane watched, astonished. It took him less than three minutes to devour every morsel she'd placed on his plate. His aquamarine eyes were wild, his sensual mouth glistening with juices from the roast, his hands—oh, God, he started licking his fingers, his firm pink lips sucking, and her temperature rose ten degrees.

Elation filled her. Although he'd never admitted that he'd been ordered to eat only bread, she'd figured it out herself. Each night while she'd dined, he'd shot furtive glances her way, watching her eat, eyeing the food with blatant longing, and a time or two, she'd heard his stomach rumble.

"More." He shoved his platter at her.

Happily, she complied. And a third time, until he sat back, sighing.

His eyes were different, she mused, watching him. There was something new in them, a welcome defiance. She decided to test it.

"I don't think you should eat anything but old bread in the future," she provoked.

"I will eat what I deem fit. And 'tis no longer bread."

Her lips ached from the effort of suppressing a delighted smile. "I don't think that's wise," she pushed.

"I will eat what I wish!" he snapped.

Oh, Aedan, Jane thought lovingly, fighting a mist of joyous tears, *well done*. One tiny crack in the façade, and she had no doubt that a man of Aedan's strength and independence would begin cracking at an alarming rate now that it had begun. "If you insist," she said mildly.

"I do," he growled. "And pass me that wine. And fetch another flagon. I feel a deep thirst coming on." Centuries of thirst. For far more than wine.

Aedan couldn't get over the pleasure of eating. Sun-warmed tomatoes, sweet young corn drenched with freshly churned butter, roasts basted with garlic, baked apples in delicate pastry smothered with cinnamon and honey. There were so many new, intriguing sensations! The fragrance of heather on the autumn breeze, the salty rhythmic lick of the ocean when he swam in it to bathe each eve, the brush of soft linen against his skin. Once, when no one had been in the castle, he'd removed his clothing and stretched naked on the velvet coverlet. Pressed his body into the soft ticks. Pondered lying there with *her,* but then he'd caught a rash from the coverlet that had made the part of him between his legs swell up. He'd swiftly dressed again and not repeated that indulgence. Unfortunately, the rash lingered, manifesting itself at odd intervals.

There were unpleasant sensations, too: sleeping on the hard, cold floor whilst she curled cozily in the overstuffed bed with the beastie. The tension of watching the lass's ankles and calves as she sauntered about. The sickness he felt in his stomach when he gazed upon the soft rise of her breasts in her gown.

He'd seen much more than that, yestreen, when the audacious wench had tugged a heavy tub before the fire and proceeded to fill it with pails of steaming water and sprinkle it with herbs.

He'd not comprehended what she was doing until she'd been as naked and rosy-bottomed as when she'd arrived at the castle a fortnight past, and then he'd been too stunned to move.

Feeling strangely nauseous, he'd finally gathered his wits and fled the hall, chased by the lass's soft derisive snort. He'd warred with himself on the newly laid terrace, only to return a quarter hour hence and watch her from the shadows of the doorway where she couldn't see him. Swallowing hard, endeavoring to slow his breathing, to stop the thundering of his blood in his veins, he'd watched her soap and rinse every inch of her body.

When his hands were trembling and his body aching in odd places, he'd closed his eyes, but the images had been burned into his brain. Thirteen more days, he told himself. Less than a fortnight remained until he could return to his king.

But with each day that passed, his curiosity about her grew. What did she ponder when she sat before the hearth staring into the flames? Why had she no man when the other village women did? Why did she watch him with that expression on her face? Why did she labor so over her letters? Why did she want him to touch her? What would come of it, were he to comply?

And the most pressing question of late, as his thoughts turned less often to his king and more often to that puzzling pain between his legs or the hollow ache behind his breastbone:

How long would he be able to resist finding out?

Nine

"What are you writing?" Aedan asked casually, his tone implying that he cared not what she replied, or even if she did.

Although her heart leapt, Jane pretended to ignore him. They sat in chairs at catty-corner angles near the hearth in the great hall; she curled near a table and three bright oil globes, he practically inside the hearth atop the blaze. He'd been surreptitiously watching her across the space of half a dozen feet for over an hour, and his question was the first direct one he'd asked of her since arrival at Dun Haakon that didn't concern castle matters. Concealing a smile, she continued writing as if she hadn't heard him:

He rose from the chair so abruptly that it toppled over, crashing to the floor. His aquamarine eyes glittering with desire, he ripped the sheaf of papers from her hands and threw them aside. He towered

*over her, his intense gaze seeming to delve into her
very soul. "Forget these papers. Forget my question. I want you, Jane," he said roughly. "I need
you. Now." He began to strip, unlacing his linen
shirt, tugging it over his head. He pressed a finger
to her lips when she began to speak. "Hush, lass.
Doona deny me. 'Tis no use. I will have you this
night. You are mine, and only mine, for all of ever,
then yet another day."*

*"Why another day?" she whispered against his
finger, her heart hammering with nervousness and
anticipation. She'd never been with a man before,
only dreamed of it. And the dark Highlander standing before her was every inch a dream come to life.*

*He flashed her a seductive grin as he unknotted
his plaid and let it slip down over his ~~taut buttocks~~
lean, muscular hips. Bracing his hands on the arms
of her chair, he lowered his head toward hers. "Because not even forever with you will be enough to
satisfy me, sweet Jane. I'm a greedy, demanding
man."*

"I said what are you writing?" His voice was tight.

*His hard body glistened bronze in the shimmering
light of dozens of oil globes. "I can't resist you,
lass. God knows I've tried," he groaned, his voice
low and taut with need. "I think about you day and
night, I can't sleep for wanting you. 'Tis a madness
I fear will never abate."*

Jane swallowed a dreamy sigh and paused, quill poised
above the paper. She arched a brow at him, outwardly
calm while inwardly melting. His eyes flashing in his dark
face, he coiled tensely in his chair, as if he might leap up
at any moment. And pounce. *Oh, if only!*

"Why do you care?" she said with a shrug, trying to
sound nonchalant. She was sick of being patient. She

knew that the presence of the villagers, the laboring with his hands on what had once been his home, and his nocturnal spying upon her in the bath were beginning to take a toll. She'd been wise to take a passive role for the past two weeks, but it was time to be more proactive. She had twelve days, and she was *not* going to lose him.

"You do nothing without purpose," he said stiffly. "I merely wish to know your purpose in practicing your letters so faithfully each eve."

Jane pressed her quill to parchment again:

> *He tugged her up from the chair, crushing her body against the hard length of his own. Gazing into her eyes, he deliberately rocked his hips forward so she could feel his ~~huge cock~~ need. Hard and hot, ~~his impressive erection~~ he throbbed, pressing through the thin silk of her gown . . .*

Jane blew out a breath of pure sexual frustration—writing love scenes sure could be sheer torture for a girl with no man of her own—and placed the quill aside. Sexpot promptly jumped onto the small side table and attacked the feather, shaking it violently. Rescuing the quill before the kitten shredded yet another one, she hesitated before answering. She knew that one inadvertent misstep might drive him back into his rigid shell. He'd made it clear he would never permit her to touch him. She had to find a way to coax him to touch her.

"I'm not practicing my letters. I write stories."

"What kind of stories?"

Jane stared at him hungrily. He was so damned sexy sitting there. Only yesterday he'd taken to wearing a plaid for the first time since his arrival, saying it was cooler to work in. There he sat looking just like *her* Aedan, clad in crimson and black and no shirt. His upper body glistened with a faint sheen of sweat as he perched as close to the fire as he could get.

"You wouldn't understand any of it," she said coolly.

"Understand what?" he said angrily. "I understand many things."

"You wouldn't understand what I write about," she goaded. "I write about human things, things you couldn't possibly understand. Remember, you're not human," she pressed. "By the way," she added sweetly, "have you figured out yet what you actually *are?*" There, she thought smugly, he looked incensed. Her Aedan was a proud man and didn't like to be belittled. Over the past week he'd begun to display resentment toward anything resembling a direct order, which pleased her and made her suspect that he would defy her outright, were she to issue a firm command.

Anger and confusion warred behind his eyes. "I have been laboring with other humans. You doona know what I can and can't understand."

"*Never* read my stories," she said sternly. "They are private. It's none of your business, Aedan."

"So long as I am laird of this castle, everything is my—" He broke off with a stricken expression.

"Laird of this castle?" she echoed, searching his gaze. He hadn't even bothered to chastise her for calling him 'Aedan.'

He stared into her eyes a long moment, then said stiffly, "I meant that the villagers think I am, so if you're to live here, in what they think is my castle, you should abide by that perception, too. Or find another place to live, lass. That's all I meant," he snapped, then pushed himself angrily up from his chair. But at the doorway, he cast a glance over his shoulder so full of frustrated longing, so rife with desire, that it sent a shiver up her spine. It was plain to see that he was beginning to feel all the things he'd once felt, but couldn't understand them.

Much later, Jane scooped up her papers in one arm and Sexpot in the other. She knew *exactly* which scene of the manuscript she was working on to inadvertently leave lying about tomorrow.

Ten

The first time he kissed her slowly, brushing his lips lightly back and forth, creating a delicious sensual friction, until hers parted, yielding utterly. The second, deeper, even more intimately, and the third so possessively that it made her dizzy. His silky tongue tangled with hers. He fitted his mouth so completely over hers that she could scarcely breathe. If a kiss could speak, his was purring, "You are mine forever."

Subsequent kisses blended, wet and hot and intoxicating, one into another until her head was reeling. She trembled, burning with the scorching heat of desire.

She whimpered when he traced the curve of her jaw, down her neck to the top of her breast. His touch evoked a blend of lassitude and adrenaline that made her feel strong and weak at the same time. Soft and supple, yet close to aggression. Hot and needy and achy.

His aquamarine eyes promised lovemaking that would strip bare far more than her body. Gently slipping the sleeves of her gown from her shoulders, he bared her breasts to his hungry gaze. The chill air coupled with the molten promise in his eyes made her breasts feel tight and achy. When he lowered his dark head and captured a ~~pouty~~ nipple in his mouth, she whimpered with pleasure. When he buried his face between her breasts, slipping her gown down over her hips, she pressed ~~her honeyed womanhood~~ against him, clinging.

His lips seared her sensitive skin. He scattered light kisses across her tummy, nipping and nibbling, then dropping to his knees before her.

She could barely stand, her knees so weak with desire, and when his hot tongue pressed to her hotter flesh, lapping sweetly at her ~~passion juices~~ most private heat, she nearly screamed with the exquisiteness of it.

Jane stood in the doorway of the great hall, a smile curving her lips, watching Aedan. Fifteen minutes ago, she'd informed him that she was going to take a quick nap before beginning preparations for their evening meal. She'd headed for the bedchamber, conveniently leaving a few pages of her manuscript lying beside the hearth, as if forgotten.

He'd nodded nonchalantly, but his gaze had betrayed him by drifting to the parchment. Shortly after retiring to the bedchamber, she'd crept back to the hall. He was standing by the fire, reading so intently that he didn't even notice her standing in the shadows of the stone doorway, watching as his eyes narrowed and his grip tightened on the parchment. After a few minutes, he wet his lips and wiped beads of sweat from his forehead with the back of his hand.

"I feel quite rested now," she announced, striding

briskly into the hall. "Hey!" she exclaimed, feigning outrage that he was snooping. "Those are my papers! I told you not to read them!"

His head shot up. His eyes were dark, his pupils dilated, his chest rising and falling as if he'd run a marathon.

He shook the parchments at her. "What are these . . . these . . . *scribblings?*" Vengeance demanded in a voice that should have been firm but came out sounding hoarse. His chest felt tight, that heavy part of him betwixt his legs . . . *och, Christ, it hurt!* Instinctively, he palmed it through the fabric of his kilt to soothe it, hoping the pain would diminish, but touching it only seemed to make it worse. Appalled, he removed his hand and glared at her. She seemed to find the gesture quite fascinating.

Jane cornered him and tried to grab the papers from his hand, but he held them above his head.

"Just give them back," she snapped.

"I doona think so," he growled. He stood looking at her, her jaw, her neck. Her breasts. "This man you write of," he said tensely, "he has dark hair and eyes of my hue."

"So?" she said, doing her best tö sound defensive.

" 'Tis *me* you write about," he accused. When she made no move to deny it, he scowled. " 'Tis in no fashion a proper woman might write—" He broke off, wondering what he knew of proper women when he knew naught of female humans but what he'd learned from her. He studied her, trying to think, which was immensely difficult with parts of his body behaving so strangely. His breath was too short and shallow, his mouth parched, his heart pounding. He felt intensely alive, all his senses stirring . . . demanding. *Starving for touch.* "This pressing of the lips of yours makes one feel as if one is"—he glanced back at the papers—"burning with the scorching heat of desire?" He, who'd long been cold, ached to feel such heat.

"Yes—if a man's any good at it," she said archly. "But

you're not a man, remember? It probably wouldn't work for you," she added sweetly.

"You doona know that," he snapped.

"Trust me," she provoked. "I doubt you have the right stuff."

"I doona know what this right stuff of yours is, but I know that I am formed like a man," he said indignantly. "I look as all the villagers do." He thought hard for a moment. "Verily, I believe I am more well formed than the lot of them," he added defensively. "My legs more powerful," he said, moving his plaid to display a thigh for her. "See? And my shoulders are wider. I am greater of height and girth, with no excess fatty parts." He preened for her, and it was everything she could do not to drool. More well formed? Sheesh! The man could drive the sales of *Playgirl* right through the roof!

"*What*ever," Jane said, purloining one of her teenage niece Jessica's most irritating responses, guaranteed to provoke, issued in tones that implied *nothing* he could say or do might interest her.

"You would do well to not dismiss me so lightly," he growled.

They stared at each other for a long tense moment, then he glanced back at the parchment. "Regardless of whether I'm human or no, 'tis plain from your writings that you wish me to do such things to you." His tone challenged her to deny it.

Jane swallowed hard. Should she pretend to order him not to? Should she concede? She was on tricky terrain, uncertain what would push his buttons just a teeny bit further. He was so close to falling on her like a ravening beast—and God, how she wanted him to! As fate would have it, her very indecision provoked him correctly. As she hesitated, nibbling on her lower lip, a thing she did often while thinking hard, his gaze fixed there. His eyes narrowed.

"You *do* wish me to," he accused. "Else you would have denied it outright."

She nodded.

"Why?" he asked hoarsely.

"It will . . . er, make me happy?" she managed lamely, twirling a strand of hair around her finger.

He nodded, as if that were a fine excuse. After a moment's hesitation he croaked, "You wish this now? At this very moment? Here?" He fisted his hands, half crumpling the parchment. His blasted voice had risen and dropped again like a green lad's. He felt incomparably foolish. Yet . . . also as if he faced a moment of ineluctable destiny.

Jane's throat constricted with longing as she gazed at him. She wanted him every bit as much as she needed to breathe and eat. He was necessary to the care and feeding of her soul. She nodded, not trusting herself to speak.

Vengeance stood motionless, his mind racing. His king had ordered that he not permit a human female to touch him. But he'd said nothing about *Vengeance* touching a human female. There was this thing inside him, this great gnawing curiosity. He wondered if there was such a thing as "burning with the scorching heat of desire," and if so, just how it might feel. "If I do this, you may not touch me," he warned.

"I can't touch you?" she echoed. "That's *so* ridiculous! Don't you wonder why your king made up that idiotic rule?"

"You will do as I demand. I will do this thing as you have written, only if you vow not to touch me."

"Fine," she snapped. *Anything* to get his hands on her. She'd cheerfully acquiesce to being tied to the bed, if she must. Hmmm . . . intriguing thought, that.

When he stepped forward, she tipped her head back and gazed up at him.

He glanced swiftly at the parchment, as if committing it to memory. "First, I am to brush my lips lightly across yours. You are to slightly part yours," he directed.

"I think we can play it by ear," she said, leaning minutely nearer, praying fervently that he wouldn't change his mind. She felt she might combust the moment he touched her, so long had she ached to feel his hands on her body.

He glanced back at the parchment with a look of alarm and confusion. "You mentioned naught of ears in your writing. Am I to do something with your ears, too?"

Jane nearly whimpered with frustration. Snatching the parchment from his hands, she said, "It's a figure of speech, Aedan. It means we'll figure it out as we go along. Just begin. You'll do fine, I promise."

"I'm merely trying to ascertain we both know our proper positions," he said stiffly.

The hell with proper, Jane thought, moistening her lips with her tongue and gazing up at him longingly. The last thing she wanted from him was *proper.* "Touch me," she encouraged.

Warily, he leaned closer.

Jane swayed forward, drawn like a magnet to steel. She wouldn't be satisfied until she was clinging to him like Saran Wrap. Although she was forbidden to out and out touch him, once he touched her, she certainly could press against him.

But still, he didn't move.

"Would you please just *start* already?"

"I am not quite certain I know what your 'most private heat' is," he admitted reluctantly. What was happening to him? he wondered. Complying with his demand, she was not touching him, but the tips of her breasts nearly brushed his chest, he could feel the heat of her body, and an alarming urgency flooding his.

"I'll help you find it," she assured him fervently.

"You're too short," he hedged.

It took Jane two seconds to retrieve the small footstool from beside the hearth, plop it down at his feet, and stand on it. It put them nose to nose, a mere inch apart.

She stared at him, heart thundering.

And he stared silently back.

Their breath mingled. His gaze dropped from her eyes to her lips. Back to her eyes, then lips again. He wet his lips, staring at her.

Jane kept her hands behind her back so she wouldn't touch him, knowing he'd use it as an excuse to leave. It was intensely intimate, such closeness without actually touching. And the way he was looking at her—with such raw hunger and heat!

A small sound escaped her. He answered in kind, then looked startled by his involuntary groan. Jane scarcely dared breathe, waiting for him to move that last tiny half inch. His dark, raw sexuality coupled with his innocence of lovemaking was an irresistibly erotic combination. The man was an expert lover, of that she had no doubt, yet it was as if it were his first time ever, and each touch would be an undiscovered country to him.

She gave a quarter inch, and he met her halfway.

His lips touched hers.

God, they were cold! she thought, stunned. Icy.

God, she was warm, he thought, stunned. Blazing.

Fascinated, Vengeance pressed his mouth more snugly to hers. He knew he was supposed to use his tongue somehow, but wasn't certain he understood the mechanics of it.

"Taste me," she breathed against his lips. "Taste me like you would lick juice from your lips."

Ah, he thought, understanding. Mesmerized by the softness of her lips, he touched the tip of his tongue to them, running it over the seam, and when her lips parted, he tasted her like he was trying to remove a bit of cream from the center of a pastry.

She was infinitely sweeter.

And then his body seemed to take over, to understand something he didn't, and with a hoarse groan, he plunged his tongue into her mouth and crushed her against him, locking his arms securely behind her back. But that wasn't good enough, he quickly decided, he needed her head just so, so he slipped his hands deep into her hair and clamped her face firmly, kissing her until they were both breathless.

It was incredible, he marveled, stopping to stare at her. He touched a finger to his own lips; they were warm.

And she got prettier when he kissed her! he thought, awestruck. Her lips got all swollen and cushy-looking, her eyes sparkled like jewels, and her skin grew rosy. *He'd* done that to her, he thought, with pride. He could make a lass prettier merely by pressing his lips to hers. 'Twas a gift his king had ne'er told him he possessed. He wondered how much prettier she'd get if he touched his lips to her in other places.

"You are lovely, lass," he said in a voice utterly unlike his own normal tone—indeed, it came out raspy and thick. "Nay, doona speak, I haven't finished."

He pressed his lips to hers again, swallowing her words. With butterfly light touches, his thumbs caressed smooth circles on the delicate skin of her neck, along the line of her jaw, and over her face. Then he drew back and ran his fingers lightly over her face, as if he were blind, absorbing the feel of every plane and angle from the downy soft brows to the pert nose and high bones of her cheeks, from the shape of her widow's peak to the point of her chin.

Her soft, lush lips.

When he rested a finger there too long, she gently sucked the tip of it, and heat lanced straight down to his groin. The vision of her lips closed full and sweetly around his finger near made him crazed . . . reminded him of something else, long forgotten, something a lass might do that was sweeter than heaven. His breath caught in his throat.

She stared at him, her amber eyes glowing, wide, trust-

ing, her lips around his finger. It made him nearly mad
with some kind of pain in his breast.

Taking her face between his hands, he kissed her as if
he could suck the heat of her right into his body, and
indeed, it seemed he did. "I want to touch you 'til your
skin smells of me," he growled, not knowing why. "Every
inch of it."

But Jane understood. It was a purely male way of mark-
ing his territory, loving his woman until she bore his
unique scent from head to toe. She whimpered assent into
his mouth, her hands curled into fists behind her back
because it was killing her to not touch him.

Then he lifted her from the stool, crushing her against
him completely, holding her weight as if she were light
as a feather, and his hard, hot arousal pressed into the vee
of her thighs.

I'm dying, Vengeance realized dimly. The feel of her
body against that swollen part of him that seemed to have
never recovered from whatever rash he'd caught from the
coverlet burned and throbbed angrily. He must be dying,
because no man could withstand such pain for long.

Mayhap, he thought, once he'd undressed her as she'd
directed in her parchments, he could doff his tartan, too,
and she might tell him what was wrong with him.

But nay—he would press his lips to hers a few more
times, for she might see the thing betwixt his legs and be
disgusted. Flee him. For now, he was warm . . . so warm.
He slipped his hands from her hair and down over her
breasts. He shuddered, once, twice, and three times, before losing complete control of himself.

He had no idea what he'd done, lost to a madness of
sorts, until he stood looking at her as she perched atop
the small stool naked, tatters of her dress scattered across
the floor. He had no clear memory of ripping her gown
away, so urgent and fierce had his need been to bare her
completely to his touch.

"Did I hurt you?" he demanded.

Jane shook her head, her eyes wide. "Touch me," she encouraged softly. "Find my most private heat. You may look for it wherever you wish," she encouraged, eyes sparkling.

He circled her slowly. She didn't move a muscle, merely stood naked on the stool as he marveled over every inch of her. And when he returned to face her, he sucked in a breath. She'd done it again—grown more beautiful. Her eyes were filled with some lazy, dreamy knowing he could only guess at. Glittering and sleepy and desirous, her skin flushed from head to toe.

He reached out with both hands and gathered the firm, plump weight of her breasts in his palms. They felt sweet, so sweet. Their eyes met and she made a soft mewing sound that shivered through him.

"Kiss—"

"Aye," he said instantly, knowing what she wanted, and lowered his head to the soft pillows of her breasts. Unable to comprehend why he wanted it so badly, he closed his lips over first one nipple, then the next. Unknowing why he did it, his hand slipped between her soft thighs, sought the warmth and wetness. . . .

And images assaulted him—he was someone else—a man who knew much of soft thighs and heated loving. A man who'd lost everything, everyone:

"Aedan, please dinna go!" the child sobbed. "At least wait 'til Ma and Da come home!"

"I must go now, little one." The man crushed her in his arms, brushing helplessly at her tears. " 'Tis only for five years. Why you'll be but a lass of ten and three when I return." The man closed his eyes. "I left a note for Ma and Da . . ."

"Nay! Aedan. Dinna leave me," the child said, weeping as if her heart would break. "I love you!"

"Ahhh!" Vengeance roared, thrusting her away, clutching his head with both hands. He bellowed wordlessly, backing away until his spine hit the wall.

"Aedan! What is it?" Jane cried, jumping off the stool and scurrying toward him.

"Doona call me that!" he shouted, his palms clamped to his temples.

"But Aedan—"

"Haud yer wheesht, woman!"

"But I think you're remembering," she said frantically, trying to touch him, to soothe him.

Another wordless bellow was his only reply as he raced from the hall as if all the hounds of hell were nipping at his heels.

Eleven

Above all else, it would be unwise to seek the company of female humans or permit them to touch you.

It would be unwise.

How had he overlooked such nonspecific phrasing?

It would be unwise. Vengeance didn't feel particularly wise at the moment. Nor did he intend to eat bland food, nor did he intend to circumvent Kyleakin because "it might be best."

Just as he'd begun to suspect, his king had, in truth, not issued a single order at all.

How and when did I meet him? Vengeance wondered for the first time. Had he been born in Faery, pledged to the king from birth? Had he met him in later years? Why couldn't he *remember?*

Vengeance sat in silence beside the gently lapping ocean, slapping the blade of a dirk against his palm.

Fairies didn't bleed. They healed too quickly.

Vengeance made a fist around the blade.

Blood seeped from his clenched hand and dripped down the sides. He spread his fingers and studied the deep cuts.

They remained deep, oozing dark crimson blood.

A harsh, relieved breath escaped him.

How old was he? How long had he lived? Why could he not recall ever changing? Why did humans gray on their heads, yet Vengeance remained unchanged?

Nothing changes in Faery.

If he never went back, would his long black hair one day silver, too? Strangely, the thought appealed to him. Thoughts of a child rose unbidden in his mind. He imagined hugging one of the wee village lasses in his arms, wiping away her tears. Teaching her to climb trees, to make boats out of wood and sail them in the surf, bringing her a litter of mewing kittens whose mother had died birthing them.

"Who am I?" Vengeance cried, clutching his head.

It occurred to him that, in truth, mayhap the right question was—who had he once been?

Jane watched him from the front steps of the castle. He sat with his back to her in the deepening twilight, clutching his head, staring out to sea. Blood was smeared on one of his hands, dripping down his arm. Suddenly he stood up, and she caught a gleam of silver as he flung a blade, end over end, into the waves.

A salty breeze whipped at his hair, tangling the dark strands into a silken skein. His plaid flapped in the breeze, hugging the powerful lines of his body.

He seemed dark and desolate and strong and utterly untouchable.

Jane's eyes misted. "I love you, Aedan MacKinnon," she told the wind.

As if the wind eagerly whisked her words down the front lawn to the sea's edge, Aedan suddenly turned and looked straight at her. His cheeks gleamed wetly in the fading light.

He nodded once, then turned his back to her and walked off down the shore, head bowed.

Jane started after him, then stopped. There'd been such desolation in his gaze, such loneliness, yet a great deal of anger. He'd turned away, clearing demonstrating his wish to be alone. She didn't want to push him too hard. She couldn't even begin to understand what he was going through. She was elated that he was remembering and equally anguished by the pain it was causing him. She watched, torn by indecision, until he disappeared around a bend in the rocky shoreline.

Twelve

He didn't come back for three days. They were the most agonizing three days of Jane Sillee's life.

Daily, she cursed herself for pushing him too far too fast. Daily, she berated herself for not going after him when he'd begun walking down that rocky shore.

Daily, she lied to the villagers when they came to work, assuring them he'd only gone to see a man about a horse and would return anon.

And nightly, as she curled with Sexpot in the bed that was much too large for just one lonely girl, she prayed her words would prove true.

Thirteen

It was the middle of the night when Aedan returned.

He awakened her abruptly, stripping the coverlets from her naked body, sending Sexpot flying from the bed with a disgruntled meow.

"Aedan!" Jane gasped, staring up at him. His expression was so fierce that her sleep-fogged brain cleared instantly.

He stood at the foot of the bed, his dark gaze sweeping every inch of her nude body. He'd braided his hair. His face was dark with the stubble of a black beard, shadowing his jaw. In the past few weeks, he'd lost weight, and although he was still powerfully muscular, there was a leanness to him, a dangerously hungry look, like a wolf too long alone and unfed in the wild.

He didn't say a word, just stripped off his shirt and kicked off his boots, then moved toward her.

She never would have believed it of herself, but he radiated such barely harnessed fury that she scuttled back against the headboard and crossed her arms over her breasts protectively.

"Och, nay, lass," he said with silky menace. "Not after all the times you've tried to get me to touch you. You willna naysay me now."

Jane's eyes grew huge. "I-I—"

"Touch me." He unknotted his plaid and let it fall to the floor.

Jane's jaw dropped. "I-I—" she tried again, and failed, again.

"Is something wrong with me?" he demanded.

"N-no," she managed. "Uh-uh. No way." She swallowed hard.

"And this?" He palmed his formidable erection. "This is as it should be?"

"Oh," Jane breathed reverently. "Absolutely."

He eyed her suspiciously. "You're not just saying that, are you?"

Jane shook her head, her eyes wide.

"Then give me those kisses of yours, lass, and be quick about it." He paused a moment, then added in a low, tense voice, "I'm cold, lass. I'm so cold."

Jane's breath hitched in her throat and her eyes misted. His vulnerability melted her fears. She rose to her knees on the bed and extended her hands to him.

Never breaking eye contact, staring into her eyes as if the invitation in them was all that was sustaining him, he placed his hands slowly in hers and let her pull him onto the bed, where he knelt facing her.

She glanced down at their entwined hands, and his gaze followed. Her hands were small and white, nearly swallowed by his work-roughened and tan fingers. She flexed her fingers against his, savoring the first *real* feel of holding Aedan's hand. Until that moment, she'd only touched him in her dreams. She closed her eyes, savoring every bit of it, drinking the experience dry.

She opened them to find him regarding her with expectancy and fascination.

"Sometimes I think I know you, lass."

"You do," she said, with a little catch in her voice. "I'm Jane." *Your* Jane, she longed to cry.

He hesitated a long moment. Then, "I'm Aedan. Aedan MacKinnon."

Jane stared at him wonderingly. "You've remembered?" she exclaimed. "Oh, Aedan—"

He cut her words off with a gentle finger against her lips. "Does it matter? The villagers think I am. You think I am. Why should I not be?"

Jane's heart sank again. He still didn't recall.

But . . . he was here, and he was willing to let her touch him. She would take what she could get.

"Jane," he said urgently, "am I truly as a man should be?"

"*Everything* a man should be," she assured him.

"Then teach me what a man does with a woman such as you."

Aw, her heart purred. The look in his eyes was so innocent and hopeful, nearly masking the ever-present despair in his gaze.

"First," she said softly, raising his hand to her lips, "he kisses her, like so." She planted a sweet kiss in his palm and closed his fingers over it. He did the same with both her hands, lingering over the sensitive skin of her palm.

"Then," she breathed, "he lets her touch him *all* over. Like this." She slid her hands up his muscular arms and into his hair. Removing his leather thong, she combed her fingers through the plait until it fell dark and silky around his face. She laid her palms against his face, staring into his eyes. He was still beneath her touch, his eyes unfocused.

"More," he urged, a stray tomcat, starved for touch.

"And she touches him here," she said, skimming his shoulders, the muscles of his back, down over his lean hips, and back up his magnificent abs and muscled chest. Unable to resist, she dropped her head forward against his chest and licked him, tasting the salt of his skin.

A rough groan escaped him, and the heat of his arousal throbbed insistently against her thigh.

Jane whimpered at the contact and pressed against him. She tasted his neck, his jaw, his lips and buried her hands in his hair. "Then, he brushes his lips—"

"I know this part," he said, sounding pleased with himself.

Fitting his mouth to hers, he kissed her; a deep, starving soul-kiss, and dragged her hard against his body.

The feel of her naked body against his bare skin made his head swim. Made him burn. Made him tremble with wonder. He'd never known . . . he'd never suspected what pleasure was to be found in touch. The feel of her wee hands on his body made him hotter than any fire could and brought him crashing to his knees inside himself.

She'd said that he was fashioned as a man should be, and she touched him as if she desperately craved his body. He liked that. It made him feel . . . och, just feel and feel and *feel*.

He nibbled and suckled at her lips, then plunged his tongue deeply, thrusting. His body moved to a rhythm, innate and primal. She went supple in his arms, dropping back onto the bed, and he followed, stretching his body atop her lush softness. "Christ, lass, I've ne'er felt aught such as you!" Intoxicated, he kissed her deeply, his silky hot tongue tangling with hers. When she shifted her legs beneath him, the swollen part of him was suddenly flush between her thighs, and he thrust against her instinctively. She raised her hips, pressing back, and he thought he would die from such sensation. He cupped her bottom and pulled her more firmly against him. Digging his fingers into the softness of her bare bottom filled him with a wild and fierce sensation—an urge to possess, to hold her beneath him until she wept with pleasure. Until he shuddered atop her. Images came to him then:

Of a man and a woman rolling naked across a bed. Of the firm pistoning motion of a man's hips, of slender ankles and calves raised near a woman's breasts, of the musky scent of skin and bodies, the sweat and rawness and heat of—

"You have no clan. You have no home," the dark king said.

"Nay, I do! I have clan all o'er the Highlands. My Highlands. My home." 'Twas the thought of his clan that sustained him. Along with yet a more exquisite thought— but the king had tried to steal that other, most important thought from him, so he'd built a tower of ice around it to keep it safe.

"Everyone in your clan died a hundred years ago, you fool. Forget!"

"Nay! My people are not dead." But he knew they were. Naught but dust returned to the Highland soil.

"Everyone for whom you cared is dead. The world goes on without you. You are my Vengeance, the beast who serves my bidding."

And then the darker images, as the pain, the unending pain began . . . and went on and on until there was nothing left but a single frozen tear and ice where once had beat a heart that held the hallowed blood of Scottish kings.

He pushed her away, roaring.

Stunned, Jane fell back on the bed. Bewildered by his abrupt leave-taking, she stammered, "Wh-what—" She shook her head, trying to clear it, to understand what was happening. One minute he'd been about to make wildly passionate love to her, the next he was five feet away, looking horrified. "Why did you stop?"

"I can't do this!" he shouted. "It hurts too much!"

"Aedan—it's just—"

"Nay! I canna, lass!" Eyes wild, trembling visibly, he turned and stormed from the bedchamber.

But not before she saw the remembering in his dark gaze.

Not before she saw the first faint hint of awareness of who and what he really was.

"Oh, you know," she breathed to the empty room. "You *know*." Chills shivered down her spine.

And he did. She'd seen it in his gaze. In the pain etched in his face, in the stiffness of his body. He'd left her, moving like a man who'd gone ten rounds in the ring, whose ribs were bruised, whose body was contused from head to toe.

She had the sudden terrifying feeling that he might leave her, that he might simply go back to his king so that he wouldn't have to face what he would now have to face.

"Aedan!" she cried, leaping up from the bed and chasing after him.

But the castle was empty. Aedan was gone.

Fourteen

Jane trod dispiritedly into the castle, shoulders slumped.
It had been a week since Aedan had left, and she had only
two more days before . . . before . . . whatever was going
to happen would happen. She had no idea exactly what
would come to pass, but she was pretty certain he would
be gone from her, forever.

No longer in this castle. No longer even in her dreams.

Leaving her to a life of what? Only memories of dreams
that *nothing* could ever compare to.

Reluctant to go in search of him, in case he returned
only to find *her* gone, she'd been crying off and on for a
week. She'd barely been able to converse with the villagers when they came to labor every day. The castle was
progressing, but to what avail? Both the "laird and lady"
would likely be gone in a matter of forty-eight hours, no
more. How she would miss this place! The wild rugged
land, the honest, hard-working people who knew how to
find joy in the smallest of things.

Sniffing back tears, she mewed for Sexpot who, for a change, didn't come scampering across the stone floor, tail swishing flirtatiously.

Glancing around with tear-blurred eyes, she drew up short.

Aedan was sitting before the hearth, feet resting on a stool, with Sexpot curled on his lap.

As if him being there, petting the "wee useless beastie" wasn't astonishing enough, he'd propped the painting Elias had unearthed weeks ago against the table facing him and was staring at it.

She must have made some small sound, because without looking up, hand moving gently over the kitten's silvery fur, he said, "I walked about the Highlands a bit. One of the villagers was kind enough to ferry me to the mainland."

Jane opened her mouth, then closed it again. Such intense relief flooded her that she nearly crumpled to her knees. She still had two more days to try. *Thank you, God*, she whispered silently.

"Much has changed," he said slowly. "Little was familiar to me. I lost my bearings a time or two."

"Oh, Aedan," she said gently.

"I needed to know this place again. And . . . I suppose . . . I needed time."

"You don't have to explain," she hastened to assure him. The mere fact that he'd returned was enough. She'd nearly given up hope.

"But I do," he said, his staring fixedly at the portrait. "There is much I need to explain to you. You have a right to know. That is," he added carefully, "if you still wish to share these quarters with me."

"I still wish to share these quarters, Aedan," she said instantly. Some of the tension seemed to leave his body. How could she make him understand that she wished not only to share "quarters" but her body and her heart? She longed to share *everything* with him. But there was something she had to know, words she needed to hear him say. "Do you know who you are yet?" She held her breath, waiting.

He looked at her levelly, a bittersweet smile playing faintly upon his lips. "Och, aye, lass. I am Aedan MacKinnon. Son of Findanus and Mary MacKinnon, from Dun Haakon on the Isle of Skye. Born in eight hundred ninety-eight. Twice-removed grandson of Kenneth McAlpin. And I am the last of my people." He turned his gaze back to the portrait.

His words, delivered so regally, yet with such sorrow, sent a chill up her spine. "Beyond that, you need only tell me what you wish," she said softly.

"Then I bid you listen well, for I doona ken when I may have the will to speak it again." That said, he grew pensively silent and gazed into the fire, as if searching for the right words.

Finally, he stirred and said, "When I was a score and ten a . . . man of sorts . . . came to this castle. At first, I thought that he'd come to challenge me, for I was heralded the most powerful warrior in all the isles, descended from the mighty McAlpin himself. Mayhap I was a bit pleased with myself." He grimaced self-deprecatingly.

"But this man . . ." He trailed off shaking his head. "This man—he terrified even me. He looked like a man, but he was dead inside. Ice. Cold. Not human, but human. I know that doesn't make sense, but 'twas as if all the life had been sucked from him somehow, yet still he breathed. I feared he would harm my people and mock me while doing so. He was great and tall and wide, and he had powers beyond mortal."

When he paused, lost in his memories, Jane whispered, "Please go on."

He took a deep breath. "Ma and Da were away at sea with all my siblings but the youngest. I was here with my wee sister." He gestured to the portrait. "Rose." He closed his eyes and rubbed them. "Although I may have suffered my share of arrogance, lass, all I'd e'er wished for was a family, children of my own, to watch my sisters and brothers grow and raise their children. To live a simple life. To be a man of honor. A man that when he was laid into the earth, others said, 'He was a good man.' Yet on that day, I knew that such things would ne'er come to pass, for the man who'd come for me threatened to destroy my entire world. *And I knew he could do it.*"

Eyes misting, Jane hurried to him, sank onto the footstool, and placed a gentle, encouraging hand on his thigh.

He covered it with his own, staring at the portrait.

After a few moments, he turned his head and looked at her, and she gasped softly at the anguish in his eyes. She wanted to press kisses to his eyelids as if to somehow kiss all the pain away, to make sure nothing ever hurt him again.

"I made a deal with the creature that if he left my clan in peace I would go with him to his king. His king offered a bargain and I accepted, thinking five years would be a hellish price to pay, wondering how I could withstand five years in his icy, dark kingdom. But it was ne'er five years, lass—'twas five hundred. Five hundred years and I forgot. I *forgot.*" He slammed a fist down on the arm of the chair. Thrusting the kitten at her, he leaped to his feet and began pacing. Sexpot, alarmed by the sudden commotion, scampered off for the calm of the bedchamber.

"I became just like him—the one who'd come to claim me. I lost all honor. I became the vilest of vile, the—"

"Aedan, stop," Jane cried.

"I became that thing I despised, lass!"

"You were tortured," she defended. "Who could survive five centuries of . . . of . . ." She trailed off, not knowing what he'd withstood.

Aedan snorted angrily. "I let them go. To escape the things that the king did to me. I let memories of my clan, of my Rose, go. The more I forgot, the less he punished me. God, there are things in the dark king's realm, things so . . ." He snarled, shaking his head.

"You *had* to forget," Jane said intensely. "It's a miracle that you survived. And although you might think you became this Vengeance creature who came for you—you *didn't*. I saw the goodness in you when I came here. I saw the tenderness, the part of you that was aching to be a simple man again."

"But you doona know the things I've done," he said, his voice harsh and deep and unforgiving.

"I don't need to know. Unless you wish to tell me, I need never know. All I need to know is that you are never going back to him. You're never going back to him, are you?" Jane pressed.

He said nothing, just stood there, looking lost and full of self-loathing. His head bowed, his hair curtaining his face.

"Stay with me. I want you, Aedan," she said, her heart aching.

"How *could* you? How could anyone?" he asked bitterly.

Ah, she thought, understanding. He hungered to be part of the mortal world—that was why he'd come back to Dun Haakon, rather than turning to his king—but he felt he didn't deserve it. He feared no one would want him, that once she knew what he'd been, she would cast him out.

He glanced at her, then quickly glanced away, but not before she saw the hope warring with the despair in his gaze.

Rising to her feet, Jane held out her hand. "Take my hand, Aedan. That's all you need do."

"You doona know what these hands have done."

"Take my hand, Aedan."

"Begone, lass. A woman such as you is not for the likes of me."

"Take my hand," she repeated. "You can take it now.

Or ten years from now. Or twenty. Because I will still be standing here waiting for you to take my hand. I'm not leaving you. I'm *never* leaving you."

His anguished gaze shot to hers. "Why?"

"Because I love you," Jane said, her eyes filling with tears. "I love you, Aedan MacKinnon. I've loved you forever."

"Who are you? Why do you even *care* about me?" His voice rose and cracked hoarsely.

"You still don't remember me?" Jane asked plaintively.

Aedan thought hard, pushing into the deepest part of him, that part that still was iced over. A hard shining tower of ice still lay behind his breast, concealing something. Helplessly, he shook his head.

Jane swallowed hard. It didn't really matter, she told herself. He didn't have to remember their time together in the Dreaming. She could live with that, if it meant she could spend the rest of her life here on this island with him. "It's okay," she said finally with a brave smile. "You don't have to remember me, as long as you—" She broke off abruptly, feeling suddenly too vulnerable for words.

"As long as I what, lass?"

In a small voice, she finally said, "Do you think you could care for me? In the way a man cares for his woman?"

Aedan sucked in a harsh breath. If only she knew. For the week he'd wandered, he'd thought of little else. Knowing he should do her the favor of never returning, yet unable to stay away. Dreaming of her, waking to find his arms reaching for nothing. Until, unable to push her from his heart, he'd faced his memories. Until, scorning himself for a fool, he'd returned to Dun Haakon to force her to force him to leave. To see the disgust in her gaze. To be sent away so he could die inside.

But now she stood there, hands outstretched, asking him to stay. Asking him to make free with her body and heart.

Offering him a gift he hadn't deserved but vowed to earn.

"You wish that of me? I who was scarce human when you met me? You could have any man you wished, lass. Any of the villagers. Nay, even Scotia's king."

"I want only you. Or no one. Ever."

"You would trust me so? To be your . . . man?"

"I trust you already."

Aedan stared at her. He began to speak several times, then closed his mouth again.

"If you refuse me, I'll cast myself into the sea," she announced dramatically. "And *die*." Not really, because Jane Sillee wasn't a quitter, but he needn't know that.

"Nay—you will not go to the sea!" he roared. Eyes glittering, he moved toward her.

"I am so lonely without you, Aedan," Jane said simply.

"You truly want me?"

"More than anything. I'm only half without you."

"Then you are my woman." His words were finality, a bond he would not permit broken. She had given herself to his keeping. He would never let her go.

"And you'll never leave me?" she pressed.

"I'll stay with you for all of ever, lass."

Jane's eyes flared, and she looked at him strangely. "And then yet another day?" she asked breathlessly.

"Oh, aye."

"And we could have babies?"

"Half dozen if you wish."

"Could we start making them now?"

"Oh, aye." A grin touched his lips; the first full grin she'd ever seen on his gorgeous face. The effect was devastating: It was a dangerous, knowing grin that dripped sensual promise. "I should warn you," he said, his eyes glittering, "I recall what it is to be a man now, lass. *All* of it. And I was ever a man of greedy and demanding appetites."

"Oh, please," Jane breathed. "Be as greedy as you wish. Demand away."

"I will begin small," he said, his eyes sparkling. "We will begin with the pressing of the lips you so favor," he teased.

Jane flung herself at him, and when his arms closed around her, she went wild, touching and kissing and clinging to him.

"Woman, I need you," he growled, slanting his mouth across hers. "Ever since I remembered the things a man knows, all I could think of were the things I ached to do to you."

"Show me," she whimpered.

And he did, taking his sweet time, peeling away her gown until she was naked before him, kissing and suckling and tasting every inch of her.

He experienced no difficulty whatsoever finding her most private heat.

Fifteen

The Unseelie king sensed it the precise moment he lost his Vengeance. Though the mortal Highlander had not yet regained full memory, he loved and was loved in return.

The king's visage changed in a manner most rare for him; the corners of his lips turned up.

Humans, he thought mockingly, *so easily manipulated.* How infuriated they would be if they knew it had never been about them to begin with, and, indeed, rarely was. His Vengeance had performed precisely as he'd expected, twisting his three nebulous suggestions, and with obstinate human defiance, aiding the king in his aim.

Eons ago, a young Seelie queen for whom he suffered an unending hunger had escaped him before he'd been through with her.

She'd not risked entering his realm again.

His smile grew. If he must stoop to conquer, it was not beneath him.

He swallowed a laugh, tossed his head back, and let

loose an enraged roar that resonated throughout the fabric
of the universe.

The Seelie queen heard the dark king's cry and permitted
herself a small, private smile.

So, she mused, feeling quite lovely, he had lost and she
had won. It made her feel positively magnanimous. Sipping the nectar from a splendidly plump dalisonia, she
rolled onto her back and stretched languidly.

Perhaps she should offer the dark king her condolences,
she mused. After all, they were royalty, and royalty did
that sort of thing.

After all, she had won.

She could simply duck in and back out, gloat a bit.

And if he tried to restrain her? Keep her captive in his
realm? She laughed softly. She'd beaten him this time.
She'd *proved* that she was stronger than she'd been mil-
lennia ago when he'd caged her for a time.

Feeling potent, inebriated on victory, she closed her
eyes and envisioned his icy lair . . .

The iciness of his realm stole her breath away. Then she
saw him and inhaled sharply, sucking in great lungfuls of
icy air. Her memory had not done him justice. He was
even more exotic than she'd recalled. A palpable darkness
surrounded him. He was deadly and powerful, and she
knew from intimate experience just how inventively, ex-
haustively erotic he was. A true master of pain, he understood pleasure as no other could.

"My queen," he said, his eyes of night and ice glittering.

Even as powerful as the Seelie queen was, she found
it impossible to gaze into his eyes for more than a moment. Some claimed they'd been emptied of matter and
pure chaos spooned into the sockets.

She inclined her head, averting her gaze ever so slightly. "It would seem you have lost your Vengeance, dark one," she murmured.

"It would seem I have."

When he rose from his throne of ice, and rose and rose, she caught her breath. Not quite fairy, his blood mixed with the blood of a creature even the Fae hesitated to name. His shadow moved unnaturally as he rose, slithering around him, wont to move independently of its host.

"You seem unperturbed by your defeat, dark one," she probed, determined to savor every drop of her victory. "Care you not that you have lost him? Five centuries of work. Wasted."

"You presume you knew my aim."

The Seelie queen stiffened, staring into his eyes for a moment longer than was wise. "Pretend not that you intended to lose. That I have been manipulated." Her voice dripped ice worthy of his kingdom.

"Loss is a relative thing."

"I won. *Admit* it," she snapped.

"I doubt you even knew what game we played, young one." His voice deep, silky, and mesmerizing, he mocked, "Did you come to gloat because my defeat made you feel powerful? Did it make you feel safe in seeking me? Careful. A being such as I might be inclined to find you reason to condescend. To sink to my depths."

"I have sunk to nothing," she hissed, feeling suddenly foolish. She *was* young by his standards, for the king of darkness was ancient—sprung from the loins of an age she'd heard of only in legend.

He said nothing, merely regarded her, his stare a palpable weight. She repressed a shiver, remembering her last excursion to his land. She'd nearly failed to summon the power to leave. But, she conceded with a thrill of sexual anticipation so intense that it nearly brought her to her knees, she'd not quite been in a hurry to leave the dark king's dangerous bed. And therein lay double the danger . . . .

"I came to offer my condolences," she said coolly.

His laughter alone could seduce. "So offer, my queen." He moved in a swirl of darkness. "But offer that for which we both know you hunger. Your willing surrender."

And when he was upon her, when he had gathered her up and his great wings began to flap, she let her head fall against his icy breast. Darkness so thick it had texture and taste surrounded her. "Never."

"Heed me well, light one, the only thing you are never with me—is safe."

Much later, when he possessed her completely, a full blood moon stained the sky above the Highlands of Scotland.

Aedan made love to Jane like a man who understood that this day, this moment, only this *now* was securely in the palm of his hand, taking her with the passionate urgency of a tenth-century Scotsman who knew not what tomorrow might bring: brutal war, drought, or crop-destroying tempest. He made love like a drowning man, desperate for the surety of her body—she was his shore, his raft, his harbor against what storms may come.

And then he made love to her again.

This time, with exquisite gentleness. Brushed his lips against the warm hollow of her neck in which her heartbeat pulsed. Kissed the slopes of her breasts, tasted the salt of her skin and the sweetness of her passion glistening between her thighs, and flexed himself deep within her innermost warmth.

He became part of her. Finally, he knew the kind of loving that made two one and understood Jane was his world. His ocean, his country, his sun, his rain, his very heart.

And that sleek, iced citadel behind his breastbone—

behind which he'd concealed from the dark king that which was most infinitely precious to him—cracked at the foundations and came crashing down.

And he finally remembered what he'd sealed away there . . . his Jane.

"Jane, my own sweet Jane," he cried hoarsely.

Jane's eyes flew wide. He was buried deep within her, loving her slowly and intensely, and although he'd called her name aloud many times during the loving, his voice sounded different this time.

Could it be he'd finally remembered all of it? All those years they'd spent together in dreams, playing and loving and dancing and loving?

"Aedan?" His name held the question she was afraid to ask.

Framing her head with his forearms, he stared down at her. "You came to me. I remember now. You came when I slept. In the Dreaming."

"Yes," Jane cried, joyous tears misting her eyes.

There were no words for a time, only the soft sounds of passion, of a woman being thoroughly loved by her man.

When finally she could catch her breath again, she said, "You were with me always. You watched me grow up, remember?" She laughed self-consciously. "When I was thirteen, I nearly dreaded seeing you because I was so gawky—"

"Nay, you were no such thing. You were a wee lovely lass, I watched your womanhood ripening and saw what you would become. I ached for the day you would be old enough that I could love you in every way."

"Well, you didn't have to wait *quite* so long," she voiced a long-harbored complaint. *"Mmm,"* she added, gasping, when he nipped her nipple lightly with his teeth. "Do that again."

He did. And again, until her breasts felt ripe and exquisitely sensitive. Then he rubbed his unshaven cheek lightly against her peaked nipples, creating delicious friction.

"I claimed you when you were ten and eight," he managed finally.

"Like I said—long. I was ready way before then. I was ready by sixteen . . . *ooh!*"

"You were a wee babe still," he said indignantly, stilling inside her.

"Don't stop," she gasped.

"Doona think for a minute 'twasn't difficult for me to naysay you. 'Twas that my mother insisted all her sons forgo impatience and give a lass time to be a child before having bairn of her own."

"Please," she whimpered.

Heeding her plea, he thrust without cease, and she cried out his name over and again, digging her fingers into his muscular hips, pulling him as deep as she could take him.

He kissed her, taking her cries with his lips until her shudders subsided.

"Have you had time enough, wee Jane?" he asked later, when she lay drowsy and sated in his arms. "We may have made one this very day, you ken."

Jane beamed. His shimmering eyes were again a warm tropical surf in his dark face, his lips curved with sensuality and tenderness. He'd finally remembered her! And she might have his baby growing inside her. "I want half a dozen at least," she assured him, smiling.

Then she sobered, touching his jaw lightly. "When I was twenty-two, the dreams seemed different. They became repeats of earlier dreams."

His jaw tensed beneath her hand.

"I lost you," she said. "Didn't I?"

"The king discovered I was gaining strength from my dreams. He prevented me from joining you there," Aedan said tersely.

She inhaled sharply. "How?" she asked, not certain she wanted to know.

"You doona wish to know, and I doona need to speak of it. 'Tis over and done," he said, his eyes darkening.

Jane didn't press, and let it go, for now, knowing the time would come when he would need to speak of it, and she would be there to listen. For now, she would wait while Aedan became fully Aedan again.

He smiled suddenly, dazzling her. "You were my light, wee Jane. My laughter, my hope, my love, and now you will be my wife."

"*Ahem,*" she said pertly, "if you think you're getting off with that lame proposal, you have another thought coming."

He laughed. "Your headstrong nature was one of the first things I favored in you, lass. So much fire, and as cold as I was, your tempers kept me warm. Saucy like my mother, demanding like my sisters, yet tender of heart and weak of will when it comes to passion."

"Who are you calling weak?" she said, with mock indignation.

Aedan gave her a provocative glance from beneath half-lowered lids. " 'Tis obvious you have a weakness for me. You spent the past fortnight trying to seduce me—"

"Only because you'd forgotten me! Otherwise *you* would have been chasing *me* around!"

Certain of it, she scrambled from beneath him and slipped from the bed, then dashed out into the great hall. Sure enough, he followed, stalking her like a great greedy dark beast.

And when he caught her . . .

And when he caught her, he made wild, passionate love to her. Celestial music trumpeted from the heavens. ~~Celestial music trumpeted from the heavens.~~ *(It did. I swear.) Rainbows gathered to shimmer above Dun Haakon. Heather bloomed, and even the sun's brilliance paled in comparison to the luminosity of true love.*

And when he proposed again, it was on bended knee, with a band of gold embedded with tiny heart-shaped rubies, as he vowed to love her for all of ever. Then yet another day.

Excerpted from the unpublished manuscript
Highland Fire by Jane ~~Sillee~~ MacKinnon

Epilogue

"Don't forget the latest chapter, Aedan," Jane reminded as he slipped from their bed. "I missed last week, and Henna said they're going to storm the castle if I don't let them know what's going on with Beth and Duncan."

"I won't forget, lass." Donning shirt and plaid, Aedan picked up the parchments from the sidetable. He glanced at the top page.

> *She held her breath, waiting for him to kiss her, knowing that she would never be the same once she'd tasted the passion of his embrace. Her braw Highlander had fought valiantly for the Bruce and had come home to her wounded in body and heart. But she would heal him . . .*

"You know, the men say that since their wives have been reading your tales they're much more . . . er, amorous," Aedan told her. Downright bawdy, the men had actually said. Insatiable. Plotting ways to seduce their men at all hours. Her stories had the same effect on him. Reading one of her love scenes never failed to make him hard as a rock. He wondered if she suspected that before delivering her pages to the eager women, he stopped in the tavern where the husbands listened, with much jesting and guffawing, as he read the most recent installment. Although they made sport of the "mushy parts," not one of them failed to show each Tuesday when he made his weekly trip to the village. Last week, three of them had come looking for *him* when he'd failed to appear with that week's installment.

"Really?" Jane was delighted.

"Aye," he said, grinning. "They thank you for it."

Jane beamed. As he pulled on his boots, she reminded him, "Oh, and don't forget, I want peach ice, not blueberry."

"I willna forget," he promised. "You've got the entire village making your favored dish. I vow when the spring thaws come and they can't make your icy cream they may go mad."

Jane smiled. She'd been unable to resist teaching the villagers a few things that she deemed reasonably harmless. It wasn't like she was advancing technology before its time. Pushing the drapes aside, she glanced out the window behind the bed. "It snowed again last night. Look—isn't it beautiful, Aedan?" she exclaimed.

Aedan pulled the drapes back over the window and tucked the covers more securely around her. "Aye, 'tis lovely. And damned cold. Are you warm enough?" he worried. Without waiting for her reply, he stacked several more logs on the fire and banked it carefully. "I doona want you getting out of bed. You mustn't catch a chill."

Jane made a face. "I'm not *that* pregnant, Aedan. I still have two more months."

"I willna take any chances with you or our daughter."

"Son."

"Daughter."

Jane's laughter was cut off abruptly when he took her in his arms and kissed her long and hard before leaving.

At the doorway he paused. "If 'tis a lass," he asked softly, "do you think we might name her Rose?"

"Oh, yes, Aedan," Jane said softly. "I'd like that."

After he left, Jane lay back against the pillows, marveling. Seven months had passed since her arrival at Dun Haakon, and although there'd been some difficult moments, she wouldn't have traded it for anything in the world.

Aedan still had a great deal of darkness inside him, of times and things he rarely discussed. There had been somber months while he'd grieved the loss of his clan. Then finally, one morning she'd come down from their new bedchamber above-stairs and found him hanging the old portraits in the great hall. She'd watched him, praying he wouldn't have that stark expression in his eyes. When he'd raised his head and smiled at her, her heart had soared.

" 'Tis time to honor the past," he'd told her. "We have a rich history, lass. I want our children to know their grandparents."

Then he'd made love to her, there in the great hall. They'd rolled across the floor, paused for a heated interlude on the table, and ended up, she recalled, blushing, in a most interesting position over a chair.

All of her dreams had come true. The village women waited with bated breath for the latest "installment" of her serial novel. They lapped up every word, savoring the romance, and the magic of it spilled over into their hearth and home. And no one ever complained about purple prose or typos.

She was a storyteller with an eager audience, a mother-to-be, had a milking cow of her own, reasonably hot water, the scent of her man all over her skin, and she slept each night held tightly in the arms of the man she loved.

Dreamily, she sighed, resting her hand on her tummy. Sexpot gave a little pink-tongued yawn and snuggled closer beside her.

Life was *good*.

Author's Note

My younger sister has long entertained me with Silly Jane Jokes. What is a Silly Jane Joke? Elizabeth is so glad you asked!

A carpenter asked the very curvaceous Silly Jane to help him. He'd hurt his foot and needed someone to climb up the ladder and retrieve his bucket of paint from the top. But Silly Jane was no fool. She knew that he just wanted to look up her dress and see her panties when she climbed it. So she tricked him. She took her panties off first.

This story is a work of fiction. Any resemblance between Silly Jane and Jane Sillee is purely coincidental. Really.